P9-DTG-096

TIME OF DEATH
REBEL REVEALED

josh anderson

Rebel Revealed
Time of Death: Book #5

Written by Josh Anderson

Published by EPIC Press™
PO Box 398166
Minneapolis, MN 55439

Printed in the United States of America.

Cover design by Dorothy Toth
Images for cover art obtained from iStockPhoto.com
Edited by Ramey Temple

LIBRARY OF CONGRESS CATALOGING-IN-PUBLICATION DATA

Anderson, Josh.
Rebel revealed / Josh Anderson.
p. cm. — (Time of death ; #5)
Summary: After learning that he's more intertwined with the mysterious Seres than he could have ever imagined, Kyle sets off on a collision course with Ayers. The hunt for his nearly invincible enemy forces Kyle to consider exactly how far he's willing to go to set the time stream back on its proper course
ISBN 978-1-68076-068-2 (hardcover)
1. Time travel—Fiction. 2. Traffic accidents—Fiction.
3. Life change events—Fiction. 4. Interpersonal relations—Fiction.
5. Conduct of life—Fiction. 6. Guilt—Fiction. 7. Self-acceptance—Fiction.
8. Young adult fiction. I. Title.
[Fic]—dc23

2015935827

EPICPRESS.COM

To Brett,

Thank you for giving me this chance, and for making it fun.

CHAPTER 1

outside of time

SIMYON FROWNED AS HE WATCHED HIS PEOPLE work. He watched them as they struggled, in silence, to move enormous metal plates across the landscape. The inside of each curved piece was nearly black. The material was the strongest, heaviest steel their mills could make. The outside of each segment of steel was still wrapped with thick mulberry branches, and there were silkworms clinging to the leaves—their only food source.

Despite the backbreaking nature of the work, disassembling the tunnel was much faster than building it. This made Simyon nervous. He pulled off the green handkerchief he wrapped around his forehead like a headband and dabbed the sweat away.

He walked across the dirt, over to where the Old Man sat, as he did, day after day, watching the work unfold. There was a long standing agreement between the two of them that Simyon would handle any issues among his people without the Old Man's interference, so long as his people always did what the Old Man asked. The problem now was that the directive had shifted and Simyon's people had begun to panic.

Simyon sat down on the grassy hill next to the Old Man, overlooking the progress. "They need to know what they're doing, sir."

"Isn't that obvious?" the Old Man answered.

"They want to know why?" Simyon said. "What happens when they're done?"

Even if he and his people were essentially slaves, the idea of finishing their work concerned them all much more than their servitude.

"Well, I don't envision building the tunnel again," the Old Man said. "It sounded like a good solution. Kept things in line. But I'm done with all that."

"Because of the rebel?" the young man asked.

"There've been rebels before," the Old Man said. "I've cut your brother's people a lot of slack over the generations. But, it's gotten out of hand . . . " He shook his head as he looked off at the thousands of workers down the hill from them. "We all answer to someone, y'know?"

"But, what'll happen?" the young man asked.

The Old Man shrugged. "Here? Or there?"

"Both."

"If we stop pulling up the tunnel, or if we don't?" the Old Man asked, not that the fate of the tunnel was up for debate. Simyon's people had removed thousands of years of steel already.

"I don't know," Simyon said frustrated, dabbing his face with his green handkerchief again. Every conversation with the Old Man went in circles like this.

The Old Man shrugged. "I don't know either."

Simyon looked at him and shook his head. "How can you just get rid of it when you don't know what's going to happen?"

"Y'know, the great kings on the other side, they would build these deep moats around their castles," the Old Man said. "To keep out anyone who wasn't supposed to get in."

"Isn't that what the tunnel does?" Simyon asked, knowing already where the Old Man was going.

"It was supposed to," the Old Man said. "But, I neglected to consider that a motivated enough person, well, they're just going to build a raft and get across that moat. And eventually that person will bring others. And, well, then you don't have any protection at all."

"No one's gotten through, though," Simyon said. "I've kept my word. We've done everything you asked. And now, my people are scared. They don't know what's going to happen when the tunnel's gone. What do I tell them?"

"Tell them what you think," the Old Man said. "What you believe."

"Real helpful," Simyon said, pounding the ground in front of him with his foot.

The Old Man gave him that half finger point he tended to give right before a lecture began. If whatever cold peace they'd held for generations was coming to an end, decorum wouldn't matter anymore between them, so Simyon stood up. If he wasn't going to get answers, he wasn't in the mood. He'd held up his end of the deal, but the Old Man clearly wouldn't give *him* any such assurances.

"You *do* remember that it's *your* mess that started all of this? Yours and your brother's," the Old Man asked.

Simyon swatted at the air and walked away without looking up again. He wrapped his handkerchief around his forehead and tied it in the back. He had nothing to bring back to his people. *What good were slaves if there was no labor?* they had been asking him. He walked back to the work site and picked up his shears from the sand. Dismantling the metal of the tunnel was harder work, but cutting the thick layer of mulberry from the outside of the tunnel made Simyon sad. It had been generations since he'd become an expert in cultivating the mulberry trees, growing them underneath the tunnel site, and forcing the branches to grow around the huge structure to ensure the entirety of the tunnel was covered. Seeing the branches shorn and discarded—the silkworms and their cocoons displaced—piled up in the sand, he realized that he'd have to tell his people *something* just to keep them working while there was still work to be done. He knew better than to disobey the Old Man, and while his people were feeling unsettled, there was no real gain in pushing for answers that they might not like anyway.

Taio walked over to Simyon. To someone on the other side, they would appear to be about the same age, but Taio was Simyon's great-grandson. His best friend, too. "Well?" Taio asked.

Simyon didn't answer. It had taken nearly three

hundred ninety generations to build the tunnel. But, it was clear that, even with some stalling, dismantling it would take them barely a generation. He had nothing to offer. Simyon moved closer to Taio's ear, as if he were letting him on a real secret. "You can rest easy. He means us no harm."

Taio flashed a look of relief. "But will he—?"

"I don't know," Simyon said. "We need to make more progress before I ask him that."

"Why?" Taio asked.

"You know why," Simyon said. "He won't answer me now anyway. Either way, he'd think it would *deincentivize* everyone."

Taio looked at Simyon with an exasperated look. "Why do you always start from that defeated place? Think of how everyone will feel if they know we *are* going to cross over? Can you imagine if we knew we were going to have real lives when the tunnel is gone? It would make this work tolerable. Think of seeing a smile on the face your three-hundredth generation, and our kin after that. You would be a hero, instead of—"

"Instead of what, Taio?" Simyon asked.

"You do the best you can," Taio answered after a moment, a little sheepishly.

Simyon dreaded the moment in every single one of his people's existences when it became clear to them, in no uncertain terms, that they were simply functionaries. That their endless time on the beach had a single, simple purpose. No one ever needed to be told—they each realized in their own time that their individuality did not matter one bit. No one would leave, and no one would distinguish themselves from the rest of their tribe in any kind of meaningful way. It was amazing to Simyon that despite this, he would still see shreds of joy among his people from time to time. He'd been presiding over them for too many generations, though, to share in any of it.

"He means us no harm," Simyon said again. "Please make sure every generation is aware."

"It's something, I suppose," Taio answered as he walked off in the direction of the tunnel. But, Simyon knew he was just being polite to make up for daring to insinuate the truth: that Simyon's standing among his people was as low as it'd ever been.

Simyon looked back to the hill and wondered how the Old Man could have so little regard for them after so many generations. He had watched them work for longer than it took empires to rise and fall on the other side. But, to Simyon it seemed that he had still not developed an ounce of empathy for them.

He watched as the Old Man reclined on his back in the grass, resting on his elbows, scanning the workers in front of him. *Where did he go when they slept?* Simyon wondered. When nearly everyone in every generation in their camp was asleep, Simyon would watch the Old Man walk through the thick tree line beyond the hill, only to return again before any of Simyon's people awoke. They were forbidden to follow beyond the tree line, and with only one exception, Simyon's people had always obeyed. The one who hadn't was made an example of in a way that ensured future generations would be warned off making the same mistake.

Simyon went back to snipping mulberry branches from the tunnel. There was still plenty more work before the disassembly was complete, but at his age, time always passed more quickly than he expected. Perhaps something good would come out of his next conversation with the Old Man. *Perhaps it would,* he told himself over and over again. *Perhaps it would.* He repeated the words in his head as he clipped the branches, even though in reality, his next good conversation with the Old Man would be his first.

CHAPTER 2

APRIL 12, 2005

a few minutes after the earthquake

ALLAIRE, LYING IN KYLE'S ARMS, HAD JUST FINISHED explaining her revelation that both Kyle and his father, Sillow, were Seres. This meant that Kyle was responsible for guarding the secret of time travel for the rest of his life, and for seeing to it that Ayers—also a Sere—didn't do any more damage to the universe than he already had by creating more and more unnecessary timestreams. Kyle had experienced so much since the first time he'd entered a silk blot with his original goal of saving the children of Bus #17.

If Allaire was correct, then what had been a choice for Kyle when he woke up this morning was, all of a sudden, his duty.

Allaire had spent years trying to stop Ayers's path of destruction, but ineffectively, since she was not allowed to kill him, because she believed Ayers was the lone Seres heir. Even more than protecting the universe from the damage Ayers could do, Allaire's job for nearly her entire life had been the protection of the Sere bloodline, which she'd been told was connected with the fate of humanity itself.

Allaire had explained to Kyle how, many years ago, Ayers mentioned another branch of the Sere bloodline to her but, that she'd written it off as one of his mad ravings. If the information hadn't come from Ayers, she might've realized sooner that the best explanation for everything they hadn't been able to explain so far was that Kyle himself *was* a Sere. She reasoned that Demetrius—who had been like an older brother to Allaire growing up—had a brother himself, who'd been cast off, since Seres' tradition dictated there could only be a single heir for each generation. A second heir—especially a second son—was a powerful taboo in their ancient traditions. The jettisoned brother, of course, was Sillow, Kyle's father, who grew up completely unaware of the Seres or who he really was.

Kyle had had a revelation of his own while Allaire was still stuck under the rubble, even before learning that he was a Sere. He knew now that there was too much at stake to ever walk away from everything he'd seen since he first crawled inside of a silk blot. There was Ayers running roughshod over the timestream, and the tunnel itself getting shorter and shorter, and figuring out what that meant for the fate of the universe. Until today, he'd believed there would come a point at which life became "normal" again. A time at which the Seres, and the tunnel, would become a distant thought to him. But, he knew this was his life now, too.

Since Kyle was a Sere, they could kill Ayers now without the concern of leaving the Seres without an heir. Finding and killing him, of course, would be no easy task. Not to mention the issue of twelve-year-old Ayers, plucked by older Ayers from his original timestream to live captive above a Chinese restaurant in upstate New York. The child seemed nothing like his older, bloodthirsty self, and Kyle had no idea why. And then, even as he'd thought of all of this—as he came to terms with the fact that he was now on the front lines of a war he might never win, or even understand—the one thing Kyle felt most scared about was the possibility of never seeing Allaire again. If she had died under that rubble, the look she'd given Kyle in the car, just before they'd chased Ayers into the building above the Chinese restaurant, would have haunted him forever. It was her *real* love look—not the fake one she'd drawn him in with when they first met—and Kyle was addicted to it. How could he possibly have lived without seeing that look again?

After spotting Allaire in the rubble a few minutes earlier, twelve-year-old Ayers walked through the rubble, jumping from beam to plywood board to overturned sofa. Kyle held Allaire in his arms, soaking in that look from her again. "No more of the back-and-forth," he said kissing her lips. "I'm done with that."

"What back-and-forth?" she asked with a slight look of concern.

He smiled at her. "I'm not interested in remaking any future where there's not going to be a place for *this*," he said, squeezing her gently and kissing her again. "From now on, whatever we do, it's together."

Allaire smiled and kissed him back now. "Then let's go figure out what kind of destiny you've got in store, Kyle Cash."

"First step," Kyle said, "is that, *together*, we need to decide what we're going to do with the kid."

"It *is* like he's a different person," Allaire said, nodding her head. "I mean, I knew Ayers at twelve, and—"

"You think the older Ayers keeping this younger one locked up in that room prevented him from getting crazy and violent?" Kyle asked. "Seems like being locked up would *make* you crazy, not the other way around."

"Listen, Kyle, he's playing us," Allaire said. "He knows what we have to do, and he's trying to make us change our minds."

Kyle wasn't sure what Allaire meant. "What do we *have to do*?"

"You know the answer to that, my love," she said.

Kyle shrugged. "I know we need to find the older Ayers and kill him. But—"

"But," she said, "it doesn't make sense to kill one version of him and just leave the other around to grow up into the same person?"

"He's not the same, Allaire," Kyle said. "I don't think this *child* is capable of tricking us like this."

"You realize that you're not much older than that 'child' right?" she asked with a smile. "You don't know Ayers like I do. If there's any of *that* Ayers inside of this younger one, we can't risk letting him free."

It troubled Kyle that she was able to make a joke in the same breath that she tried to convince him their only choice was to kill a twelve-year-old. "Okay," he said. "Then we keep him close. We don't have to make any final decisions now."

Kyle reached into his pocket and pulled out his silk blot. Emergency personnel would be here soon, and they needed to get out of 2005 before people started asking them questions.

Young Ayers breezed over to them, walking on a huge metal beam like it was a tightrope. "How cool is it that I found you under there?"

"Very cool," Allaire said. "I haven't properly thanked you yet . . . Thank you, Ayers."

"I always tell Mr. Ayers that kids can kick some ass too," Ayers said. "But he still never takes me with him when he leaves. He says I would blow up."

Kyle noticed a vibration in his pocket and pulled out his silk blot. "Have you ever seen this happen?" Kyle asked Allaire, holding the blot up in front of him. Young Ayers knelt down to look, too. The blot rippled in Kyle's hands. It was a slow, fluid, life-like movement, like you'd see from a sea cucumber at the aquarium.

"Ow," Ayers said, his eyes glazing over as he watched the blot move in Kyle's hands.

"What's wrong?" Allaire asked.

Ayers put his hands against his ears and squinted like he was in pain. "I'm okay, I think. It feels like a little headache."

Kyle looked at Allaire. "Little?"

Ayers bent at the knees and waited, shrinking from the pain as he held his ears. The sight of the kid in pain drove home for Kyle that they needed to explore every conceivable option before they considered harming him. A child was a child, even if he might grow up to be a sociopathic, time-weaving monster.

After a few seconds, Ayers grabbed the soft underside of his forearm and let out a yelp. He lay on the ground now and moved his head between his legs. "Please make it stop!" He was crying, his body writhing in pain.

Allaire and Kyle looked at each other. She pulled her karambit from its holster and looked around.

Kyle grabbed her wrist, laying the rippling silk blot on a metal rod at his side. The blot shook more and more violently, like something inside of it was trying to get out. "No!" Kyle said firmly.

"He's in pain," she said. "Let me help him."

Kyle shook his head, and whispered to her through gritted teeth. "He's not a stray dog, Allaire. You're not going to just put him out of his misery."

"Do you *know* what he's capable of?" she asked. "He would slit my throat without a second thought. Yours too if he didn't think he needed you to never."

"Nevering!" Kyle said, the word coming to him like a revelation. "How much do you actually know about it?"

"Not much," she answered. "The Seres always talked about it like this mythical thing. They thought that if you nevered, you'd live forever."

"That might be what's happening," Kyle said. "Let's get out of here."

Kyle held the blot and pulled it over Allaire, who cringed as she moved her body inside. Then he held it for Young Ayers to climb into. When he saw Ayers was in too much pain to even notice, Kyle picked him up and sat him on his lap, pulling the blot over both of them at once. Ayers still grabbed at both sides of his head, right over his ears, whimpering now from the intense pain.

"It's gonna be okay, kid," Kyle said, having no idea if it really would be. Nothing about Young Ayers seemed dangerous at all, but assuming they could get him through whatever was happening, there would be a moment of reckoning. As much as Kyle didn't want to face it, there was more than a bit of logic to the fact that it didn't make sense to kill the tree, only to leave the seedling around to take its place. The question they needed to answer was whether it was inevitable that *this* Ayers would grow into *that* monster.

CHAPTER 3

APRIL 12, 2005

moments later

THE NORMALLY PLACID TUNNEL VIBRATED LIKE a washing machine.

The loud reverberations shocked their ears, and they had to get used to the audible assault for a couple of minutes before they could even attempt to hear each other over the noise.

"Tell me *this* has happened before?" Kyle yelled to Allaire, even though their faces were only inches apart. He held the silk blot to her face for light, since their eyes hadn't adjusted yet to the tunnel's darkness either.

She shook her head "no."

Young Ayers looked slightly less critical now.

He'd taken his hands from his ears, and just held onto the inside of his forearm, pushing down on it as if he were applying pressure to a wound. "Hurts a lot," he whined, slowly removing the hand and looking at it.

Kyle looked and saw an old looking scar. "Where'd you get that?"

"It's new," Ayers said. "I've never seen it before. Hurts so bad."

Kyle felt Ayers's arm and noticed that there was an indent under the skin, behind the scar. It was as if someone had scooped out a piece of his bone. "How do you never, Allaire?"

"I didn't think it was real," she answered. "None of the Seres knew for sure."

"Could it explain his arm?" Kyle asked. The loud rumbling stopped suddenly, leaving the tunnel in its normal quiet.

"The two people nevering need to fuse a piece of their bones together," Ayers answered, still wincing. "And their parents need to be dead. And, if they also have the special mutation, like Kyle and me, then they can live forever. Mr. Ayers talked about it all the time. When you never, you don't belong to one timestream anymore. You belong to all of them."

Kyle looked at Ayers. He hadn't considered that the kid would have important answers for them, and he also didn't understand how a younger version of Ayers could have a scar from something the older version did. In fact, Kyle's *I Don't Understand list* was long at this point because relying on logic just didn't help him much these days. "And what about the shaking in here?"

"I don't know," Ayers answered.

"It might make sense," Allaire said. "People aren't supposed to live forever. If nevering is real, and the older Ayers did it, he might've set off something in the universe. Like an alarm, maybe."

"He'd be immortal," Kyle said, feeling defeated.

"Remember, we don't know anything for sure,"

Allaire answered. "Even Ayers doesn't have all of the answers. But, if he found your dad and nevered, he doesn't need *you* for anything anymore. I don't know how we'll ever find him if he doesn't want to be found."

"My father," Kyle said. "Ayers must have him."

Young Ayers still held onto his forearm. The look of pain on his face was less than before, but still there.

"The tracker," Kyle said, referring to the tiny device he had managed to attach to Ayers's hand before he escaped through his silk blot in the apartment above the Chinese restaurant. "I put the tracker on Ayers."

"You did? When?" Allaire asked with a smile.

"Before I let him slip away," Kyle responded quietly. Everything in the apartment had happened so quickly, but Kyle knew they'd let a big opportunity pass when Ayers got away.

"Well, we need to go to 2060 for the tracker's receiver then," Allaire said. "If he didn't take the tracker off, the receiver should tell us where he is, and hopefully lead to your father as well."

"What if we go back and stop them from nevering before it ever happens?" Kyle asked.

"That's the whole point, Mr. Kyle," Ayers said. "Once you never, it can't be undone."

"He has my father," Kyle said. "We don't have time to go to 2060, Allaire. We need to find them now and get Sillow away from Ayers."

"We have no idea where to go, Kyle," Allaire answered. "We have no idea what year they nevered in. And we may not have much time anyway. The tunnel has gotten shorter and shorter since Ayers started time weaving years ago. If it gets too much shorter, pretty soon, you and I will just be erased from history."

"I don't like that my father got dragged into this," Kyle said.

Allaire shrugged and nodded. "Then let's go get the receiver for the temporal tracker and we'll find them."

Kyle's heart thumped in his chest. She had so much knowledge, and he needed and wanted her help. But Kyle was the Sere. It *had* to be his call from here on out, and the idea of going to 2060 right now just seemed wrong. He felt a strange sensation that he had trouble ignoring. "I feel like we'll just find them," Kyle said. "Like the tunnel will tell me."

Allaire smiled at him. "I've *definitely* never seen that before."

"But I feel like I'm gonna know," Kyle said.

"At the Silo, in 2060, even if the tracker doesn't work, we have surveillance of the factory going back to the 1980s," she said. "If Ayers brought Sillow there, we'll have the tape, and it'll be time-stamped. There's surgical equipment at the factory. If they nevered, that's got to be where they did it. It's a sure thing, Kyle. The answer we need is there . . . Plus . . . " Her voice trailed off as she looked at Young Ayers.

Kyle nodded at Allaire. How could he put this

strange new sensation he was feeling over the logic Allaire was providing? he wondered. It felt strange to ignore it too, though. The feeling that he *could* get them to Sillow without the tracker was so strong, but difficult to comprehend, since he didn't *actually* know. Allaire had called it a "sure thing." He put his hand on Young Ayers's shoulder and gently nudged him forward in the tunnel toward 2060.

Logic was going to win today. But, almost suddenly, this new sense of intuition filled Kyle's mind with certainty about things he couldn't actually know. He was positive, for instance, that Ayers had nevered, and that since Kyle had denied him, Ayers had found a way to get Sillow instead and make it possible. It was one of the first times in his life Kyle had felt so sure about something he couldn't touch, or see with this own eyes. Was it learning that he was a Sere that brought this out in him? Or, Kyle wondered, was he finally learning to tune into a part of him that had been there all along?

CHAPTER 4

AUGUST 28, 2060

fifty-five years later

LIKE A MOTHER SENDING HER CHILDREN TO BED, Allaire banished Young Ayers to one of the upper platforms of the Silo almost immediately after they arrived. She sent him up with a cup of ramen noodles and asked him not to bother them.

Once his arm began to feel better, Young Ayers had been an able traveling companion, deftly making his way through the tunnel. He was quiet, but not creepily so. Kyle was actually impressed that a twelve-year-old handled himself so well around two adults. Kyle was only seven years older, but his time in prison had put an abrupt end to what was left of his childhood.

Kyle took a much-needed shower and then grabbed a Pop-Tart and a granola bar from the Silo's supply pantry, a deep well of non-perishables. For the first time, he didn't move through the Silo as if he were a guest. If he was a Sere, then the Silo was *his*.

Kyle headed up to the tech platform with all of the different monitors and computers. Allaire was already there, set up at a workstation. She nodded to him without taking her eyes off the screen.

"Bad news," she said, pointing at a map of New York City on her screen. "Temp tracker's not working. I don't know if maybe it's not sealed to his skin well, or if the receiver is being finicky, but I can only get a geographical reading, not a temporal one. I can see he's in the factory building. But I can't get anything on what year he's in."

On another screen, she has paused surveillance footage of the factory's entrance. The current image on the screen had a timestamp from 2033. Her karambit and holster were laying on a small table close to the edge of the platform. It was the first time he could remember seeing her without a weapon at arm's reach. He sat down and watched as she scanned through video for a few minutes.

It was hypnotic to watch weeks zip by on the screen without a single person entering or exiting the factory building. Kyle thought about how little he really knew about Allaire's life with the Seres behind those walls. He imagined it was a fairly limited life, but since Allaire had barely spoken about it, he really had no idea.

"How long do you think it'll take to go through all of this video and find them?" Kyle asked. "I'm worried about Sillow."

Allaire sighed. "If we work in shifts? One of us sleeps while the other scans, maybe two days to get through it all. Hopefully, we see something sooner."

"I can look too," said a voice coming from the doorway. Kyle looked up and saw Young Ayers. He walked toward them holding two cups of ramen noodles. He had a Rubik's Cube tucked under his arm. "If all three of us take turns, it'll go faster," Ayers said.

Ayers handed both noodle cups to Kyle, and Kyle put one down next to Allaire.

Kyle took a slurp of noodles from his cup and grimaced at the salty broth. "Two days is a lot of ramen . . . "

"I'm too tired to eat," Allaire said. "Ayers, please go to bed."

One of the things Kyle did know about Allaire's past was that she'd taken care of Ayers when he was very young. He imagined she'd said those words many times before after so many years caring for the Ayers from her original timestream—the Ayers who wanted her dead now.

Young Ayers backed out of the room slowly. "I know Mr. Ayers is a bad man . . . So, I want to help." They heard him bound up the stairs and watched across the Silo as he got into bed on the second-highest platform. Kyle couldn't understand how this gentle young boy could ever grow up to be an unrepentant killer. It just didn't make sense.

Kyle put his hand over Allaire's, which was holding the mouse. "You go rest too."

Allaire looked up at him with bloodshot eyes. "No. We have to—"

"I've got this," he said. "At least for tonight. I'm too wired to sleep anyway."

She kept fiddling with the mouse and the keyboard, scanning through full days in only a few seconds, slowing down on the rare occasion when someone on the screen entered the factory building. "I'm fine."

"You just had a building fall on you," Kyle said. "Go rest."

"I'm fine," she said, not looking up at him this time.

"I know what's at stake here, Allaire," Kyle said. "He has my father."

She stood up. "I know you do."

He hugged her.

“I’m sorry for being a bitch,” she said. “I’m exhausted.”

She pressed her forehead into his chest. “I’ve never had a person before. Someone who was *my* person.”

Kyle pried her head away from his chest so he could look her in the eyes. There was too much still ahead of them that it didn’t feel right to fantasize about making a life together. If Ayers was really immortal, there might be nothing they could do except watch as their timestream evaporated and the world ended. “Your person’s right here,” he said to her, leading her to the stairs that led to the bedroom platforms above them.

“I want to tell you everything,” Allaire said. “I want you to know about the life I’ve led.”

Kyle touched her face with his hand. “I want to know everything, but right now, you need to rest.”

“No,” she said, sitting down on the stairs. “I almost died, and everything about me would’ve vanished. Everything about me before I met you, at least."

Kyle saw how urgent this was to her—in the moment, way more important than getting the rest she needed. He sat down next to her.

She told Kyle everything—from her happy early memories with Dr. Browning to her life with the Seres. About her friend Demetrius, and her adversary, Rickard, who killed Dr. Browning to protect the Seres' secret. Kyle also learned exactly how taxing her altercations with Ayers had been, weaving behind him through the tunnel to different eras, but never having the license to use lethal force. At the same time, she needed to defend her own life from his attacks. Kyle had only seen a glimpse of Ayers's brutality, but Allaire had lived it day after day, chasing the boy she helped raise through the tunnel as he committed horribly vicious attacks.

She finally got to explain her marriage, and how Everett was someone she'd known for only a short time. He had been brought into the factory by

Yalé as a potential replacement when he began to mistrust Allaire. Yalé had twisted Allaire's arm to marry Everett so he could get his green card and not risk deportation to Australia if he was ever detected by authorities. While Everett had taken an immediate liking to Allaire, she had only begun to trust him at the time he was killed by an oncoming car after nearly killing Kyle on the side of the New York State Thruway.

After a while, Kyle noticed Allaire beginning to nod off, her head falling forward during brief pauses in the conversation. He took her hand and walked her up the stairs. He helped her under the covers and kissed her forehead before heading back down to the tech platform.

After four hours of scanning surveillance video of the front entrance to the factory, Kyle's eyes felt like they were coated with salt. He hadn't seen anything of note on the screen in front of him, and watching the repetition of the security footage became almost meditative. Without even letting go of the mouse, his eyes began to close, but he awoke with a shudder shortly after. He felt like he'd only been asleep for a few seconds, but his dream was so vivid, he didn't know for sure. The horrific images jarred him back to full consciousness:

Young Ayers stood over Allaire as she slept. Her karambit blade in his hand, he smiled with the same demented grin Kyle had seen on the older Ayers when he sprayed bullets from his machine gun into a crowded store. Young Ayers lifted the blade over his right shoulder and drove the knife into Allaire through the white sheet covering her, opening a gaping, diagonal hole in her torso from her shoulder down to her hipbone. Allaire's eyes opened for just a brief second with a terrified look as she watched her blood turn the sheet into a wet, red mess.

The dream felt real, and Kyle tried to take a few deep breaths to slow his heartbeat. He looked at the table across the room and was happy to see Allaire's holster there.

He looked back at the screen, which was running surveillance tapes at regular speed now that he'd stopped jogging forward at a faster speed. For a moment, he absentmindedly watched the street traffic pass by outside of the factory in footage from 2038.

Wait, he thought to himself. *Allaire's blade wasn't in its holster!*

His adrenaline already on high, Kyle leapt to his feet and bounded from the platform to the stairs. He raced toward the bedroom platform where Allaire slept right above him, hoping that he hadn't let something horrible happen while he dozed off.

CHAPTER 5

AUGUST 28 & 29, 2060

seconds later

KYLE LET HIMSELF EXHALE WHEN HE SAW THE crisp, clean white sheet covering Allaire, no sign of blood anywhere. She was sleeping on her back with her hand under the pillow.

The dream had felt so real to him. He gently pulled off her sheet and examined her sleeping body. He put his knee on the bed and gently lifted her shoulder to make sure there was no blood underneath her. As soon as he touched her, Allaire's eyes quickly popped open. As she sprung up to a sitting position, she pulled her arm out from beneath the pillow and Kyle saw her blade coming toward him.

"Allaire," he screamed as he jumped back. "Wait!" He made an acrobatic roll off of the bed.

She rubbed her eyes with her other hand, and laid the karambit next to her in bed. "What's going on?"

"You fell asleep with your blade?" Kyle asked.

Allaire swept her hair from in front of her eyes. She looked at Kyle and shrugged.

"He's twelve, Allaire," Kyle said.

She pulled Kyle on top of her and hugged him tight. "Your heart is pounding."

Kyle didn't say anything.

"I know he's twelve," she whispered to him. "But they're the same person."

Kyle felt exhausted. There hadn't been many moments to breathe since he'd first entered a silk blot, and having to make decisions that could affect the entire universe was overwhelming. Somehow, though, having to deal with the question of what to do with this younger version of Ayers felt most daunting of all. "I won't kill him, Allaire. I won't do it."

"Okay, my love," she whispered into his ear, moving her hand from his back down his body. "Okay."

He felt like he needed to explain himself. He wanted them to be on the same page. If they were really each other's "people," shouldn't they see eye-to-eye on something as critical as this? "I just—"

Allaire moved her finger up to Kyle's mouth, tracing his lips with her nail. "No more talking."

He felt her wrap her legs around him and his heart began to race again for a different reason. She kissed his neck and he lifted his chest for a moment to make eye contact with her.

"Are you still attracted to me?" she asked, with none of her normal self-assuredness. "Even though I'm an old lady?" He wasn't used to seeing her look vulnerable.

"You're more beautiful than the day I met you," he said.

"Good," she said, playfully smiling at him. She reached down and tossed the karambit to the floor below them. As it landed with a thud, she wriggled out from beneath him, gently turning Kyle onto his back.

"What about the surveillance tapes?" he asked.

"Later," Allaire said as she straddled Kyle and started undoing his belt. He looked past the headboard, up to the platforms above them. *What will we do about Ayers?* he wondered. But he put the thought as far away from him as he could after that, and gave himself to the moment.

"I don't have a condom," he whispered to her.

"I told you, no more talking," she said, pulling off his belt. She undid his zipper, then flung her black t-shirt to the floor. By the time he could even consider speaking again, his mouth was too busy, and he'd forgotten his point anyway.

Kyle woke up alone in the bed they'd shared the next morning. He tried closing his eyes again. It was the first time he'd slept completely soundly in a long time. But it only took a few seconds for his brain to wake up. His first thoughts were almost too pleasant to handle. He would give anything to go back to last night. He hadn't thought his feelings for Allaire could get any deeper, but then, after physically connecting for a night, they did. Despite anything else on his mind, Kyle felt more in love than he ever had in his life.

He sat up and tried to collect himself. Today was the day he hoped they'd figure out what year they needed to visit to find Sillow and rescue him from Ayers. Of course, for all Kyle knew, Sillow could've willingly joined Ayers in nevering and creating havoc through time. Kyle wanted to have more faith in his father, but he'd known the bad side of Sillow Cash a lot longer than he'd known the heroic side. Sillow had gotten into his share of trouble in his younger days, and Kyle had no way of knowing what Ayers promised Sillow in return for nevering.

As Kyle picked his shirt up from the ground and put it on, he heard a roaring mechanical sound. He looked over the edge of the platform and saw one of the huge door panels of the Silo sliding open. The morning light from the outside shone on Allaire and young Ayers, who were standing in the doorway as the panel opened.

He watched them for a second and saw Allaire put her hand on Ayers's back. She stepped outside with him and then pointed ahead of her. He nodded and she tapped him as he ran off.

Kyle threw on the rest of his clothes, and his shoes, and hustled down to the ground floor of the Silo. "What's going on?" he called to Allaire. "Where'd you send him?"

"I need him to get some papers from the factory," she said.

"I almost got killed out there on my own," Kyle said. He started to move outside the door, but Allaire grabbed him before he could go.

She hit a button on the wall and the panels started to close. "You can't."

He tried to twist away from her, but by the time he did, the doors were closed.

He bolted upstairs to the tech platform. When he sat down at the bank of monitors again, he flicked the setting to LIVE and saw a feed from outside the factory. There was a cluster of people camped not far from the entrance. He moved his face closer to the screen and saw that they looked like the same group of people who had tried to attack him when he'd walked from the factory to the Silo. They'd chanted a language Kyle had never heard before and tried to get his silk blot. Kyle had been lucky to get away without the chanters killing him and finding their way into the tunnel. "Dammit," he said to himself. He'd barely survived the attack with a silk blot in hand. Young Ayers wouldn't stand a chance.

He got up from the chair and headed toward the stairs. He and Allaire almost bumped into each other as she entered the tech platform, but he brushed past her. "What the hell is wrong with you?" he called behind him. "What happened to doing this together?"

"We had to do something," she said.

Kyle pivoted toward her. "They're gonna rip him apart. They're going to *eat* him! I said I wouldn't kill him!"

"I know you did," Allaire said.

Kyle shook his head at her, disappointed.

"I did it to protect us, Kyle," she said. "Don't you see that?"

At that moment, he hated that he loved her. There were times when he admired that she had the conviction to do whatever needed to be done, even the unpleasant things. And there were times like this, when she seemed only a few shades down the spectrum from a psychopath like Ayers.

Kyle pounded down the stairs and raced to the Silo's exit. He hit the button to open the door.

"Kyle, no!" Allaire screamed behind him.

As soon as the door opened enough for him to squeeze through, he was out and racing down the street after Ayers.

Kyle could hear his own breath as he sprinted toward Ayers, who was walking slowly in the middle of the deserted street, about a block ahead of Kyle. "Ayers!" he screamed when he stopped to catch his breath. "Ayers!"

The boy stopped walking and turned. A few seconds later, Kyle caught up to him.

"Hi, Mr. Kyle," the boy said, completely oblivious to any danger nearby.

"Allaire found what she was looking for," Kyle said. "You don't need to go to the factory anymore."

Ayers thought about it for a second and nodded. "Okay."

They turned around and headed back toward the Silo as Kyle wondered what he could do to keep Ayers safe if Allaire really believed their only option was to kill him. And worse, he wondered if she was right and he just couldn't see it.

They hadn't even been walking for a minute when Kyle heard footsteps behind them, then to the side. He saw two flashes of red go past, and he did a full turn, trying to figure out what was happening. Instinctively, he pulled Young Ayers closer to him by his t-shirt.

Two of the people in the red shirts were standing in front of them. They were the chanters who'd come after Kyle the last time he was out here. In back of them, he saw four more chanters. Within a few seconds, they were completely encircled. They each carried a long pole with a knife on the end of it. The people chanted and waved their makeshift spears, as they had the last time Kyle encountered them.

"*Bar . . . Bar . . . Barfoo . . . Bar . . . Bar . . . Barfoo*," they called out, over and over.

"What's happening?" Young Ayers asked Kyle. "Can we go back now?"

Two of the chanters moved next to Kyle and Young Ayers, positioning the blades of their spears only inches from their bellies.

A beautiful young woman stepped forward. Kyle recognized her as Mayor Jada from the last time he'd encountered them. "Another time weaver with you this time," she said, in her heavy accent.

"Just let us go," he said.

"You have magic silk again?" Mayor Jada asked.

"*Keellen eem eenywee*," one of the men called out. It was Bertie, the man who'd tried to kill Kyle last time.

"What's going on, Mr. Kyle?" Young Ayers asked, a fearful look on this face.

All of her people, dressed in various shades of red shirts, began chanting "*Keellen eem eenywee*," over and over. Mayor Jada stayed silent. After a few seconds, she held her hand up.

"We were reasonable last time, time weaver, and we will be reasonable again," she said to Kyle. "We just want your magic silk, and for you take us into the steel castle. Show us your way."

"I can't do that," Kyle said. "Kill me if you're going to, but just let the kid go." He hated seeing the fear on Young Ayers's face. No twelve-year-old should have to face down real danger like this. Kyle hated that Allaire was completely responsible for their predicament.

Mayor Jada stood there for a minute, not saying anything as her people chanted. "Half my group died since the last time I see you. This world you time weavers made ain't no good."

"Get eez silk," Bertie called out.

Kyle saw out of the corner of his eye that Allaire was creeping up the block. She held her karambit in her hand. He should've been relieved, but he knew now that there would unquestionably be more blood spilled today. He'd seen enough brutality for a lifetime recently.

"If he had magic silk, he'd have used it by now," Mayor Jada said to her people.

One of the chanters in the group pointed ahead, past Kyle and Ayers. Everyone turned toward Allaire, who tried to slyly tuck the karambit into the waistband of her pants. She walked in the middle of the street toward them now.

"There you are, Allaire," Mayor Jada called out. Allaire quickened her pace, but when she got within about ten feet of the chanter in the front, Mayor Jada held her hand up. "Stop there," she said.

Allaire stopped and put her hands in the air. "Jada, I need these two."

"That's not for you to say," Mayor Jada answered. "All of a sudden, you need the boy? He was going to be our dinner."

"Just let us go back," Allaire said. Kyle was concerned by how worried she looked. The ground started swaying, and everyone stopped talking for a moment.

"What's happening?" Young Ayers asked Kyle. "Is that another earthquake?"

Kyle put his hand on his shoulder. "It'll be okay."

The shaking became more violent and most of the chanters knelt to the ground to keep from being knocked off balance. Kyle considered whether this might be their best opening to get away, but it would risk all of their lives, so Kyle put his arm around Young Ayers and gently pushed him down to a kneeling position.

A few seconds later, as the violent shaking continued, Young Ayers stood up, pulled a spear from the unsuspecting hands of the chanter next to him and impaled the man through the throat, pushing the spear all the way through him. As the man fell backward, and the shaking stopped, Ayers confidently jerked the spear out of him and moved toward Jada.

Kyle turned toward Bertie to try to do the same, but the huge man shook his head and pushed the spear closer to Kyle's midsection.

Jada used the dull side of her spear to quickly

disarm Young Ayers and then pulled him close to her, whipping an ice pick from her back pocket and holding it against his throat.

"Drop your weapon, Allaire, and tell me how to get into the steel castle, or I open the boy's neck right now," Jada said, holding the ice pick up to Ayers's throat. Allaire's eyes darted between Jada and Kyle, who was stuck with Bertie and the spear pointing at his midsection.

"I'm not sure I need you anymore, Allaire," Jada continued. "Those scraps of food you gave us kept you safe for a little while, but I want the steel castle now, and there are more of us than you."

Kyle looked at Allaire. A few minutes ago, she'd sent Young Ayers out of the Silo and shut the doors, hoping the chanters would kill him. Kyle tried to speak to her with his eyes. If their hearts were really as connected as he'd felt last night, maybe he could convince her without speaking. This kid did not deserve to die just because of what he *might* become. He didn't break eye contact with her for nearly a minute.

Allaire slowly took the karambit from her waistband and held it in her hand by its handle, lowering it toward the ground.

She made the motion of tossing it off to the side, but then she lifted it over her shoulder and flung it right at Jada. The knife flew end-over-end through the air, striking Jada in the shoulder. As Jada fell backward, Allaire pulled a second karambit from a holster on her leg and ran at the shorter of the two men nearest her. She lifted the blade to strike him. "Fight, Kyle! Fight!"

The taller man lifted his homemade spear and slapped it against Allaire's forearm, jarring the blade loose before she could strike the shorter chanter. The karambit slid on the ground and stopped between Kyle and Bertie, right at their feet.

Allaire grabbed onto the long stick and tried fighting off the two men.

Kyle sidestepped Bertie's spear and dove to the ground to grab the knife.

As he was on the ground, Bertie raised the spear and brought it down toward him, but Kyle rolled away, the spear missing him by only a few inches. He stood up and dodged another lunge from Bertie's spear. Then, he sprang up and buried the blade deep into Bertie's belly.

Kyle looked over and saw Ayers straddling Jada, stabbing her over and over again in the chest with the karambit blade Allaire had thrown at her.

Kyle grabbed Ayers by the shoulder and pulled him off of her. "She's dead, Ayers."

Kyle and Ayers started running back toward the Silo, while Allaire gave one more swipe through the air with a spear causing the remaining two chanters to retreat in the opposite direction. Then, she turned to follow Kyle and Ayers back to the Silo.

The three of them walked back silently to the

Silo. Ayers clung to Allaire's karambit and examined the blade, which was now slick with blood. He'd deftly killed two of the chanters, and hadn't flinched at the brutality of what they'd just done.

Kyle had no interest in talking to Allaire right now, and had no idea what to say to a twelve-year-old kid who'd just seen—and participated in—such a brutal battle.

"Told you kids can kick some ass," Ayers said.

The chanters were among the last survivors in the city. Without a silk blot, Kyle wondered, how long would *he* last in a world like this? Allaire would have a chance virtually anywhere, because she was willing to do whatever she thought necessary. Kyle wondered whether it would be possible to fully hold onto his humanity, even if he accepted that extreme violence was necessary to survive on the front lines of the war that older Ayers had waged against time.

Kyle knew Allaire needed him—maybe because she loved him, and maybe because he helped her keep that tenuous hold on *her* humanity, after so many years of making such severe compromises with her conscience. Or maybe, it was just because he was the last Sere.

The truth was, he needed her too. Partially, because when she was underneath that fallen building, he'd felt more lost than he ever had. But also because if he was going to fulfill what he now thought was his destiny, he needed someone to remind him that saving the world wasn't always going to be pretty.

He slowed down and let her catch up to him. He took her hand in his.

"I'm sorry," she said, as Ayers ran up ahead of them, playing with Allaire's karambit as he did.

He wanted to show Allaire that this time was really different—that, like he'd said, he was done with the back and forth, and wasn't going to turn his back on her just because she'd done something he didn't like. He squeezed her hand.

"I love you," she said. "I really am sorry."

Loving her, though, didn't mean sitting idly by. "Never again . . . You want to do this by yourself, you tell me. Otherwise, when we have a decision to make, like what to do with the kid, we talk about it. We decide together.

She shook her head. "You have my word."

"Okay," he said. "You have more of those blades at the Silo?"

She nodded.

"I want you to train me," he said.

"If Ayers can't be killed, what does it matter?" she asked.

Kyle shook his head. "If he's really immortal, then we'll find some way to contain him. We'll lock him up the way he locked up the kid."

"Not to broach a sore subject, but what *are* we going to do with him?" she asked as Young Ayers reached the door of the Silo about a hundred yards ahead. "In a few years, we're going to have two psychos on our hands."

"Perhaps," Kyle said. "But maybe not. I think

we need to train him, too . . . He's a Sere, and it's my job to keep my people safe, right? Until he shows us he's dangerous, we have to treat him like family."

CHAPTER 6

SEPTEMBER 4, 2060

a week later

THE UNLIKELY THREESOME SPENT THE NEXT WEEK in the Silo, making it through about a decade of surveillance footage each day. So far, they'd seen nothing to clue them into what year they would find Ayers and Sillow. Kyle still had the nagging feeling, though, that he could *sense* how to find them, but he couldn't define exactly how.

Except for a few hours each night while Ayers slept, and Kyle and Allaire "slept," two of them trained together, while the third scanned security footage. Even Young Ayers pitched in, and every day Kyle could see Allaire's trust in him growing. He might one day become a problem for them, but he wasn't one now, and Kyle thought she might finally be coming around to the fact that they couldn't be casting off any potential allies at this point.

One afternoon, Ayers noticed something on one of the archived surveillance tapes. He called Kyle up from the kitchen area and after he watched the grainy footage three times, Kyle yelled for Allaire. "I think we got it."

Allaire quickly came downstairs to the tech platform and joined them. "When? Where are they?"

"I saw them enter the factory in 2016," Kyle answered. "But, my father, he was young. About my age."

Allaire looked like she was trying to work out the logic in her mind. "Ayers probably wanted to get to Sillow before you ever told him about time weaving."

Kyle considered what Allaire had said. The first time he ever went through a silk blot was to go visit Sillow in Flemming in 1998, when Kyle asked him to intervene in the bus crash sixteen years later. Kyle had gone back to a time before his own birth to make sure he didn't see a younger version of himself, which Kyle knew now would have disastrous results.

But, before 1998, Sillow didn't know anything about time weaving, or the bus crash. He looked young enough in the footage that he might not even know Kyle's mother yet. And, Kyle knew, this was a period of Sillow's life where he was still "playing the angles"—living in the margins of the law. It made sense that this was the version of Sillow who Ayers would be most able to convince to follow him.

Kyle went downstairs and started packing a bag—a few bottles of water for the trip through the tunnel, and some energy bars with expiration dates in 2055. It was time to go now. For a brief moment, he looked around. He'd needed this time here. He felt invested in the Seres' home base now. After all, the Silo was as much of a home as he might ever expect to have.

Young Ayers stood in the kitchen, juggling three rubber knives in front of him, laser focused on the task.

"Is there any party trick you can't do?" Allaire asked him, swiping one of the knives out of the air.

"What's a party like?" Ayers asked.

Allaire just rolled her eyes. "Like I would know . . . Grab some food and water. Let's go."

"Mr. Kyle, what are you going to do to him?" Young Ayers asked.

Kyle pulled out a silk blot. He wanted to be honest with the kid, but he just didn't know enough to say anything confidently. None of them understood what nevering really meant. "We need to get my father away from Ayers," Kyle said. "That's as far as my plan goes for now."

CHAPTER 7

NOVEMBER 30, 2016

forty-four years earlier

THEY RUSHED THROUGH THE TUNNEL AND reached the rung labeled *2016*, exiting the silk blot on the same day Kyle had seen on the surveillance video. The tunnel was louder than normal again, this time with a distant clanging sound at their backs during the entire journey.

"I'm kind of jealous that you always come out of the tunnel on the day you need to," Allaire said to Kyle as the three of them walked from the future site of the Silo to the factory. "I've had to wait around for a few months sometimes, or go in and out of the tunnel, over and over again, hoping I got closer."

"You, my dear, are not a Sere," Kyle said with a smile.

As they walked, Young Ayers went to town on his Rubik's Cube, twisting and turning so much it seemed impossible that there was a real method to what he was doing. But, by the time they reached the factory building, he'd nearly turned a jumbled cube into a finished puzzle.

As they approached the entrance to the building, Kyle glanced at Allaire and they shared a nervous look.

"He should wait out here," she said, gesturing toward the boy. She mimicked a head exploding with her hands. "In case the other Ayers is up there."

"But they've been together before," Kyle said. "In the same apartment."

"He always blindfolded me when we were in the same place," Young Ayers answered without looking up from his Rubik's Cube. "And I was never allowed out of my room when he was around . . . That's how he kept me safe."

"Alright then," Kyle answered. "You're gonna stay outside."

"When we get up there," Allaire started, "you get your father out of there and into your silk blot. I'll keep Ayers occupied."

Kyle shook his head. "We don't know what nevering's done to him, though. He could be stronger now. He could kill you. We need to face him together. Give ourselves the best chance."

"Don't worry about me," Allaire said. "I can take care of myself. I've got a blot, so I'll meet you back at the Silo in 2060. Same day we just left."

"No," Kyle said. "What if something goes wrong? What if . . . I don't know . . . the timestream gets messed up and there is no 2060 anymore? No, we can't split up. We both get out of there, or neither of us do."

Allaire shook her head at him. "You need to own this."

"Own what?" he asked.

"That *you're* the special one," she answered. "That your life matters more than mine—"

"Allaire . . . That's not—" Kyle said.

"Listen," she said. "I helped the Seres keep their precious bloodline going when most of them didn't give two shits about me. Now, the man I love is a Sere, and I need you to let me do what I've always done: protect the bloodline."

"Bullshit. We need to get in there," Kyle said. "And we don't get back into that silk blot until you, me, the kid, and my father go in together."

With that exchange still hanging in the air, they were off, while Young Ayers waited behind two dumpsters in the alley next to the factory.

Allaire and Kyle took the stairs up to the fifth floor of the factory and stood for a second catching their breath just outside a heavy metal door to the side of the elevator bank.

Kyle put his ear to the door, but it was too

thick to hear anything. "What do you think they're doing in there?" he whispered.

Allaire shrugged and pulled her blade out of its holster. "Ready to find out?"

Kyle nodded, pulling Allaire's spare karambit from his pocket. He wondered whether there was any point. If Ayers really couldn't be killed, they'd have to find a different solution. Still, it felt better to hold a weapon.

Kyle turned the knob and quietly opened the door. They tiptoed through the elevator bank and peeked around a wall. They had a clear view but were still out of sight.

They saw two hospital beds set up under bright lights. Ayers sat on the side of one of the beds, his arm hooked up to an IV. Kyle could see his eyes darting all over the place, even as he sat completely still and quiet. In the other bed, Kyle saw a man laying flat on his back, also attached to an IV, with an anesthesia mask over his face. He assumed this was Sillow. Yalé wore medical scrubs and a surgical mask, and stood over Sillow, doing something to his arm. Kyle wasn't close enough to see exactly what was happening.

Yalé's intentions had always been a mystery to Kyle, but ever since he sent his assistant, Samyra, to try to kill Kyle and Allaire, he was aware that Yalé was not an ally to them.

"We have to get in there," Kyle whispered. He wondered if the Seres would even need Sillow after whatever procedure allowed Ayers to never. *What if they discarded him like they'd been so willing to discard other people?* Kyle wondered.

They stayed low and managed to make it most of the way into the room before Ayers saw them. "Uncle," he said weakly. "Uncle!"

Yalé didn't even look up from working on Sillow's arm. "This was inevitable, Ayers. You knew that."

Ayers looked at them and slid off the hospital bed to his feet. He looked wobbly.

"Ayers, sit please," Yalé said. "The anesthetic hasn't worn off yet . . . "

Kyle saw an uneasy look in Ayers's eyes for the first time. He looked at Allaire and froze.

Yalé looked at Kyle and Allaire now. "I'll be with you in a moment. I'm just finishing stitching up your father, Kyle."

Ayers just stood there, looking uneasy and glassy-eyed. "I need to go."

"You have no reason to rush," Yalé said to him, calm as ever.

Allaire started toward Ayers with fire in her eyes. She raised her karambit in the air. Ayers stumbled as he moved backward on the tile floor, still unsteady on his feet.

Yalé pulled his surgical mask down and held his hand up, stepping into Allaire's path with an irritated look on his face. "Please, stop this nonsense."

Allaire paused for a moment, then raised her arm to push Yalé out of the way.

Yalé gently pushed her back, keeping his hand up, signaling her to stay back for a moment. He picked up a scalpel from the metal tray next to

Sillow's hospital bed and turned toward Ayers. Just as a look of shock registered on Ayers's face, Yalé began stabbing Ayers over and over. There was no passion in the overhand strikes, just a business-like determination and enough effort to pierce the skin a least an inch each time. Yalé then plunged the scalpel into Ayers's gut several times. Each time Ayers reflexively jumped back, Yalé grabbed him by the shirt and moved him closer. "Stand still, please."

Then, Yalé poked three holes into Ayers's neck, including one directly into his jugular vein.

The attack was so brutal that Kyle couldn't help but cringe. For good measure, Yalé finished with two more overhand strikes, gouging Ayers directly in his eyes before roughly pulling out the scalpel.

Other than a stunned look, Ayers stood unfazed during the entire thing. There was no blood. He didn't seem to be in any pain. Yalé tossed the scalpel back onto the tray and lifted his surgical mask over his face again, turning back to Sillow, still asleep in the hospital bed. "Like I said, there's no rush Ayers. They can't hurt you." Yalé made a point of looking Allaire straight in the eyes for a few seconds before going back to work on Sillow.

"Why are you doing this, Yalé?" Allaire called out to him.

Yalé ignored her. As Kyle stepped closer, he could see that Yalé was stitching together a three- to four-inch gash in Sillow's forearm. There were silkworms crawling on the wound and intermingling themselves in the thread. Kyle moved even closer and saw that Yalé was even stitching some silkworms inside of the skin as he closed it up.

Ayers touched some of the places where Yalé had cut him and smiled. Kyle watched as the holes quickly closed up. As they healed, each hole had a slight shine to it—the same cloudy shimmer as a silk blot. Ayers held his hand out to Allaire, offering a handshake. "Wanna be friends?"

Allaire looked at him with a combination of fire and devastation. "Fuck you."

Ayers pointed at her and laughed. "You've got no sense of humor. You never have . . . But seriously, I hope you can find something else to do with your life now, instead of chasing me around like a stalker."

Allaire walked a little closer to Ayers, but Kyle could see she was keeping her distance. No sense getting close enough to him that he could try to kill her. Even though he still looked subdued by the anesthetic, he had gotten spryer in just the few minutes they'd been there.

"I'm going to lock you up somewhere for the rest of eternity," Allaire said. "And every time I come to see you, I'm just gonna laugh, and you're going to beg me to figure out a way to undo all of this so you can just fucking die. That's a promise."

"If I want to die," Ayers said, "that'll be my decision . . . "

Kyle wondered what Ayers meant by that, since Yalé had just shown them that Ayers was now completely impervious to being hurt or killed.

"Kyle," Ayers said. "Please talk some sense into her. I bear no grudges. We part ways now, and you don't have to look over your shoulders or anything. You have my word . . . I may have won, but I'm not pushing my luck. I want to leave well enough alone and I want peace."

"You really want peace?" Kyle said. "Then prove it, and come with us."

Ayers rolled his eyes. He looked over at Yalé now. "Uncle, how much longer until this guy's ready to go?"

Yalé didn't look up from his stitching work on Sillow's arm. "Just go, Ayers. You don't need him anymore."

"I don't *need* him," Ayers said. "But I want him. It's lonely in the tunnel and Uncle Sillow is quite a funny guy. Plus, he's a Sere, just like you and me."

"Not like you," Yalé said, tying up Sillow's final stitch. He pulled his gloves off and his mask down. "He's a second son, like me. Tainted."

Kyle remembered Allaire explaining to him that,

in Sere tradition, there could not be a second heir to the Sere bloodline. "You're not taking him anywhere, Ayers," Kyle said.

"This guy on the table, he doesn't even know you," Ayers said. "He's not your father yet."

"But he will be," Kyle said. "And you're not touching him."

Ayers smiled and shrugged. "Could've been you, Kyle. You were my first choice."

"Like you said, you won," Kyle answered. "You got what you wanted. Now, leave him out of this."

"This isn't just about me, Kyle," Ayers said. "This is about *them*. This is about those like-minded individuals I find out there who just like to watch things go 'boom!' I think Sillow could've been one of those people before he got the run-of-the-mill wife, a kid, and that sad job changing bedpans at the hospital. This young Sillow's got that fighting spirit I like."

Kyle shook his head. He felt like he knew Sillow's heart enough to know that could never happen.

"Think what you want," Ayers said. "I've seen what the power of no consequences can do to someone's moral compass. It's a beautiful thing . . . See, Kyle, here's what Allaire could never understand: I'm *in* on the joke. Here's this ancient family, with this huge secret, and I'm born to be its caretaker. Except, I don't want to play by someone else's rules . . . And now, I don't have to. We don't need another Sere heir, because I'll be around forever. As long as this world exists, at least. Is he ready yet, uncle?"

Yalé turned a few dials on the machine attached to the anesthesia mask, and pulled out Sillow's IV. "He'll be fine now, as long as he rests in the tunnel."

Ayers grabbed a silk blot that was hanging on a chair between the two hospital beds and walked over to Sillow. Allaire grabbed Ayers from behind, trying to pull him backward, but he landed a hard elbow to the bridge of her nose to send her backward, stunned. Kyle came at Ayers now and punched him in the face. Unfazed, Ayers pushed him away and down to the ground with a hand to the chest.

Ayers stood over Kyle and shook his head. "You had your chance. Now stay the fuck away, or next time, I won't leave you alive."

By the time Kyle stood up, Ayers had stretched his silk blot almost completely over Sillow. Kyle could only watch as Sillow's face—younger than Kyle had ever seen in the flesh—disappeared under the blot.

Ayers made a mock salute to Allaire and Kyle, and then pulled the silk blot toward himself. "Have a swell time watching the world burn, assholes. I'm out."

CHAPTER 8

NOVEMBER 30, 2016

moments later

"LET ME GET OUT OF THESE SCRUBS BEFORE YOU kill me, please," Yalé said to Kyle and Allaire.

Kyle looked at Allaire. He had a feeling her verdict would be in line with Yalé's thinking.

"We're not here to kill you," Kyle said before Allaire could try to convince him otherwise.

"That's genuinely surprising," Yalé said, pulling off the scrubs covering a brown three-piece suit. "I've tried to kill you, and I couldn't possibly think of a reason for you to keep me alive—at least not one that I could suggest with a straight face."

Kyle sat on the edge of one of the hospital beds. He was exhausted after getting so little sleep over the past week. "I know Ayers doesn't see it that way, but for me, it's an honor to find out that I'm part of this tradition. I'm going to do better with this gift. Better than him . . . And better than you."

Yalé looked irritated. "Don't compare yourself to him. You're the son of a second son. I don't think that's ever happened inside of our bloodline before. You're entitled to nothing."

"No matter what you say, I'm not going to kill you, Yalé," Kyle said. "You might not have always used this gift we have for the right reasons, but I intend to."

"What gives *you* the right to question *me*?" Yalé asked, his usual calm starting to break.

Allaire took a deep breath and looked at Kyle. "You heard him admit he tried to kill us, right?"

Kyle nodded. "We're not—"

"Okay," Allaire said. "Okay . . . "

Yalé shook his head, and just stood there, looking irritated.

"I'm honored to be a Sere," Kyle said. "Even if you and I don't see eye to eye."

"You don't understand, son of a second son. You might have Sere blood, but you don't know what that really means. She doesn't either," he said, pointing dismissively at Allaire. "This? All of this? It's not a gift. It's a curse."

"What does that mean, Yalé?" Kyle said.

Yalé shook his head. "It means that we're holding the keys to the end of the world, and it's only a matter of time until someone drives us right off that cliff. We watch that day come closer and closer, and yet generation after generation, we make the same mistakes. We all learn, sooner or later, that things are better off when we stay out of the tunnel. But, no one's been able to resist the temptation that comes with the ability to time weave, and no one will."

"Why are you helping Ayers?" Kyle asked.

Yalé smiled and shook his head. "Because he's the rightful Sere heir, and like you, I'm just a second son. *Anything* he does is better than the *best* thing I'll ever do. Or you'll ever do."

"How can we end the curse?" Kyle asked. "Shouldn't we be trying?"

"How would I know?" Yalé answered, his eyes watery now. "I'm just a coward. I let your father out into the world because I didn't have the guts to do what was necessary when a second son was born. For thousands of years, Sere families have had a single heir. I never should've been born. Your father never should've been born. And you, the *son* of a second son, certainly should never have existed."

Kyle looked at him. Yalé had such reasonable eyes. He looked like a man who could handle anything with diplomacy. Even though he'd tried to kill them, Kyle didn't feel he was beyond their trust. "Help us, Yalé. Help us protect Ayers from himself."

"If second sons are so worthless, why does Kyle have the mutation?" Allaire asked. "He's the same as Ayers."

"People have been telling people they weren't worthy, based on birth order, or their gender, or where they were born, or what color their skin is, forever," Kyle said. "It doesn't make them right."

"Of course it does," Yalé said. "For the herder to exist, you need the sheep. For the king, you need the commoners."

"Social constructs," Allaire said. "Do you know for a *fact* you can't go into the time tunnel? Aren't you curious? You can't be *that* big of a coward."

Kyle thought he saw Yalé considering what they were saying. For a moment, Kyle wondered if they'd cracked something in him. Introduced doubt for the first time in a long while, or ever.

Then, Yalé picked up the same scalpel he used to stitch Sillow's arm, and to harmlessly puncture Ayers. He held it in his closed fist and looked right into Kyle's eyes. "I knew my place," Yalé said. "And that let me have a purpose. It let me have somewhere I belonged. And it let me survive, even though I should've never been allowed a life at all."

Kyle looked at Allaire and saw her focus was on the scalpel in his hands. She had her hand on her holster.

"A genetic mutation doesn't change the fact that you have no claim to this bloodline," Yalé said. "You're an interloper in this world, Kyle, and that won't ever change."

"Help us stop him," Kyle said, walking closer to Yalé, hoping he might have the opportunity to pull the scalpel from his hand . . . "Otherwise, none of this will matter. The bloodline will be gone, because the world will be gone . . . Allaire was lied to. Maybe you were too."

"You both think the tunnel is shortening because of Ayers," Yalé said. "But what if it's because the son of a second son has been weaving so much?" Yalé asked. "Have you ever stopped to think that maybe *you're* the problem, Kyle?"

"That's bullshit," Allaire said.

"You're so fast to write it off," Yalé said. "I'm just giving you a different way of looking at things.

It was right around the year Kyle was born that we first noticed the tunnel getting shorter. Don't be so fast to discount that."

Allaire shook her head angrily. "Kyle, he's just trying to protect Ayers by making you doubt yourself."

Yalé looked at Allaire and smiled. "You'd have no problem killing Ayers if you could, and you knew it would save other lives, but would you be as quick to kill your lover?"

Allaire started to speak, but she couldn't find words. Kyle had never considered that he himself could be the danger to the universe that they were trying to stop. He could see the conflict in Allaire, who would desperately want to write off Yalé's words, but would have no choice but to consider the possibility.

Suddenly, Yalé jerked the scalpel up to his own throat, creating a deep rupture, then let out a guttural moan as he pulled the scalpel out and did the same thing again, a few inches to the right.

Unlike Ayers, Yalé bled and bled. Within seconds, the entire front of Yalé's white dress shirt was crimson. He stabbed himself twice more before he fell to his knees. His final attempt missed, as he fell over onto his side, spurting blood out onto the factory floor for another few seconds before the last of the life inside him was completely gone.

Kyle and Allaire stood for several minutes just looking at Yalé's body without speaking. The longer they stayed silent, Kyle thought, the longer they could avoid confronting Yalé's last words, which still hung in the room like a low fog.

Finally, Allaire moved toward the body and knelt down, her knee landing just outside the radius of blood around him. She closed Yalé's eyes before standing up.

Allaire bent down once more to pick the scalpel out of Yalé's hand. She tossed it onto the hospital bed. "He was the last person alive who knew me as a child."

Together, Kyle and Allaire dragged Yalé's body to a smaller room down the hall from the main factory room which Kyle had never seen before. Inside, there was a huge brick oven—an incinerator they'd used on their dead bodies for many years. They dispassionately tossed Yalé inside, and Allaire pressed a series of buttons on a panel next to the machine, igniting a fire that quickly engulfed the body.

They turned and exited still not having said a word, and Kyle began mopping when they returned to the main factory room.

With only a few words, Yalé had made Kyle go from feeling like a potential savior of the entire universe to a villain.

"I'm going to get the kid from outside," she said. "The other Ayers isn't coming back here."

Kyle nodded and continued mopping. He wanted to be stronger. He wanted *not* to let Yalé's final words erase everything he'd learned about himself, and the way he felt about that. Finding out he was a Sere had been scary at first, but then it brought great meaning to his life for the first time . . . maybe ever. But now, all of his grand notions about trying to save the universe felt foolish to him. Kyle couldn't help but lapse back to the mindset of someone desperately trying to make up for the original tragedy he'd caused. It was like the bus crash all over again.

What if I am the problem? he thought to himself, over and over.

Meanwhile, the numbers *1997* flashed into his mind out of nowhere. He swept the meaningless thought from his head, but it kept creeping back in.

If all it took was a few words from Yalé to bring him back to earth, then he certainly wasn't cut out to be a hero, he thought to himself. *1997.*

There was no plan. Nowhere to go next. *1997.* Ayers was long gone and could've brought Sillow anywhere. Kyle sat down and put his head in his hands.

1997, Kyle thought to himself again. The number flashed brighter in his head now, the way a sparkler leaves a trail of light behind it. It was a force. It was unstoppable . . . *1997. What did it mean?* His attention shifted away from the memory of Yalé's words, as he couldn't ignore the light in front of his eyes anymore. *1997.* It was as if he could reach out and touch the numbers, even though they were clearly not *actually* in front of his face. *1997.* Was he going insane? *1997! 1997! 1997!*

He'd had this feeling earlier in the Silo, without seeing a specific year. It was almost as if he'd known this would come to him, and now, here it was. With each passing second, the numbers became brighter and brighter. By the time he heard the elevator doors opening, the image was so vivid that he could barely see in front of himself. He waved his hands in front of his face, but there was nothing to feel. *1997* was indeed just inside his head, only there for him to see.

"What the fuck are you doing?" Allaire asked, walking in with Young Ayers as Kyle was running his hands through the air in front of him.

"He was wrong, Allaire," Kyle said. "Yalé was *wrong.*"

He looked at her and she smiled. "I know he was. I'm glad you do too," she answered.

"I know what year we need to go to," Kyle said. "I know where Ayers and Sillow went. The universe. The tunnel. Something. It's talking to me, Allaire."

CHAPTER 9

NOVEMBER 30, 2016

an hour later

WHILE KYLE FINISHED CLEANING UP THE MESS in the main factory room, Allaire put together backpacks for all three of them. It was the kind of planning for a trip through the tunnel that they usually never had time for. She was able to bring extra ammo, night-vision goggles, and other accoutrements they always needed, but never had. Young Ayers explored the fifth floor of the factory, and while Kyle was too eager to get moving to do the same, he was envious and couldn't wait to explore his new home when he had the chance.

Allaire came into the main factory room and

placed the three bags on the floor near Kyle's feet. "Ready to go?"

Kyle nodded. "Where's Ayers?"

Before either of them could yell for him, Young Ayers walked into the room holding a wooden object, which he playfully swung back and forth through the air, like a tennis racket.

"What'd you find?" Kyle asked, more to be friendly than out of curiosity.

Ayers stopped swinging it and showed it to them. It looked like a decorative fraternity paddle, except the writing on it wasn't Greek. It was polished and had characters etched into it on both sides in a language Kyle had never seen before.

"Ancient Serican writing," Allaire said. "The original Seres were from a small, long-gone place called Serica and this was their language."

"Where'd you find this?" Kyle asked.

Ayers pointed to Yalé's office. "In that room over there. It was in a drawer, but it was wrapped in branches and it had bugs on it. I cleaned it off myself."

"Do you know what it says?" Kyle asked Allaire. "Can you read it?"

She shook her head.

"What about you?" he asked Young Ayers. The kid had surprised him a few times by having answers he hadn't predicted.

Ayers picked up the smallest of the three backpacks and put it on his back. "I don't know, Mr. Kyle. Sorry . . . Can I keep it, though? Please?"

Again, Kyle could sense something that he couldn't really put into words. "No."

"Please?" Ayers asked again.

Allaire scrunched her face up at him. "Let's just go Kyle, what's the diff—"

Kyle sensed that there was something more to the paddle. He felt like it was meant to stay here. "I'm sorry . . . Please put it back where you found it."

Ayers walked with his head down toward the

office, while Kyle and Allaire put on their backpacks. "Did you put rocks in these?" Kyle asked. "I hope the kid's bag isn't this heavy."

"You can handle it," Allaire answered, leaning over and kissing Kyle on the cheek. "I want to make sure we've got everything we need."

Kyle adjusted the pack to distribute the weight as comfortably as he could and then shrugged. "Of course, I can handle it."

Allaire pulled a silk blot from the spinning machine in the room and held it in front of her.

When Young Ayers returned a minute later, the three of them went outside to the alley next to the building and ducked into the blot. The clanging inside the tunnel had become so loud that they could barely hear each other over the noise. If Kyle was wrong about where they needed to go, he had no idea what their next move would be. But just as he began to doubt himself, the number flashed again in front of his eyes, as if to reassure him: *1997.*

CHAPTER 10

SEPTEMBER 29, 1997

nineteen years earlier

ALLAIRE'S THOROUGH PACKING CAME IN HANDY immediately when they needed to stake out the front entrance of the factory building. She pulled a wire hanger from her backpack and quickly got them into an Oldsmobile parked right across the street from the entrance. A few seconds later, she had the car hot-wired and the air conditioning on, too.

Kyle had the temporal tracker's receiver in his lap, watching the red light on the screen blink without moving, meaning Ayers was inside the factory building. The tracker still wouldn't confirm Ayers's temporal location, but it worked fine to pin down his geographic location.

After sitting quietly in the back seat for almost an hour fiddling with his Rubik's Cube, Young Ayers leaned forward toward the front. "What are you going to do to me?"

Kyle looked at Allaire, but neither of them said anything as the question hung there for a few seconds.

"If we didn't believe there was a way for this to turn out okay for all of us," Kyle continued. "We wouldn't be here."

"You promise?" Ayers asked.

Kyle nodded. "Yup. I do."

"Good," Ayers said. "Because remember that kids can kick some ass, too."

"I know you can," Kyle said. He thought about how Young Ayers probably had no role models at all, stuck in the single room that Ayers had put him in. Any of his positive experiences with people were likely from movies, TV, video games or books. Even the slightest bit of encouragement from him, Kyle thought, must mean the world.

The thought made Kyle feel twice as bad that he hadn't said something more reassuring about their plans for him.

"Let me show you guys how these earpieces work," Allaire said, changing the subject. "They're like walkie-talkies, but you don't need to hold them."

It was late in the afternoon when they saw Ayers and Sillow walk out of the factory's entrance and turn left toward 7th Avenue. The street had the buzz of early rush hour. Both men wore New York Mets baseball caps low over their eyes, with Ayers leading the way and Sillow following.

"They're on the move," Kyle said. He felt a surge of confidence as he watched the men walk up the block. Either Kyle's abilities really were as strong as he hoped they were, or some force wanted to lead Kyle to exactly this time and place. Either way, seeing Ayers and Sillow here in 1997 made him feel more confident that he was doing exactly what he was supposed to.

Kyle and the version of Sillow walking down the street were about the same age. Sillow was even skinnier at eighteen than he was a few years later when Kyle met him during his first trip through time.

“Let’s go,” Kyle said, once they were up the block a bit, and Allaire started the ignition. “You really think driving at rush hour is a good idea?”

“I don’t want to risk them seeing us,” Allaire said, pulling out of the parking spot onto West 38th Street.

They drove slowly up 38th following behind them as the two men continued down the block. His heartbeat already racing, Kyle jumped when he heard the roaring horn of a taxicab, the driver clearly annoyed to be stuck behind them. The driver sat on his horn and didn't let up, even when Allaire picked up the pace a bit.

At the corner, they watched as Sillow and Ayers turned left and went up 7th Avenue.

"Shit," Allaire said. "It's a one way."

Without hesitating, Kyle opened his car door. "Come on."

Young Ayers popped out in the middle of the street and Kyle corralled him to the sidewalk. Kyle looked back at Allaire who sheepishly followed right behind them, not looking back to face the taxicab, now stuck behind their abandoned vehicle and once again screaming with his horn.

"Traffic's not that bad," Allaire said. "I just forgot Seventh was a one-way street."

Once they were safely onto the sidewalk, Kyle started running to keep from losing Ayers and Sillow. He weaved around pedestrians, with Allaire and Young Ayers right behind. Their blue Mets caps made them easier to spot in the thick crowd, but it was hard to move quickly through such a dense sea of people. He glanced down at his tracker and watched them move down the street. As he looked up, Kyle slammed into a UPS delivery driver carrying a heavy box, bouncing off him without losing his balance. Several times he lost a visual on the two blue hats only to spot them again a few seconds later. They were coming up on Times Square, though, where it would be even more difficult to keep tracking them.

If they were going to catch up, Kyle thought, he needed to move faster. But every time he tried, it seemed like he wound up behind a mother with a stroller, or an elderly couple. By the time he reached 40th Street, Kyle had lost them. The red dot representing Ayers was gone from the tracker too. He stopped and waited for Allaire and Young Ayers to catch up. Kyle felt relieved that she'd stayed with the boy, making sure not to lose him in the crush of pedestrians.

"Let's keep going," she said. "Maybe you'll have another feeling."

It felt good that Allaire believed in him. Kyle peeked over a railing going down to the subway, and then out at the mass of people. He spotted four more subway entrances within a couple of hundred feet of them. There were likely more people in one square block here than in all of Flemming. The chances of finding them before they showed up again on the tracker were minimal.

"How many more people will be dead by the time we find him?" he wondered out loud. "They're down in the subway now, or else they'd be on the tracker . . . And why the matching caps?"

"To keep anyone from noticing them, probably," Allaire said.

Kyle looked across the street at a newsstand. "Come with me a second."

They waited for the light and walked across the street. He picked up a copy of the Daily News from a newsstand and flipped it open to the sports section. "Mets play tonight?" he asked the guy inside the kiosk, as he looked for the information in the paper.

"Who cares?" the guy answered in a foreign accent. "Baseball's boring."

"What time is it?" Kyle asked him.

"Ten to seven," he answered.

Kyle put the paper down, and walked toward Allaire and Young Ayers. Behind him, he heard the guy in the newsstand complaining that he'd looked at the paper and not bought it.

"Let's go to the ballgame," Kyle said.

Allaire looked at him skeptically. "Is this another feely thing, like you knew to come to 1997? Or . . . ?"

"We just lost them right here by the entrance to the Seven-Train, which goes to Shea Stadium. And they were wearing Mets caps . . . " Kyle said, realizing it didn't sound quite as compelling when said it as it did when he thought it.

"And . . . ?" Allaire asked.

"And, we don't have anything else to go on," Kyle said. "C'mon, I'll buy everyone hot dogs."

"Are they good?" Young Ayers asked. "I've never tried one."

CHAPTER 13

SEPTEMBER 29, 1997

an hour later

ALLAIRE PLACED THE RECEIVER IN KYLE'S EAR AS they stood outside of Shea Stadium, where the New York Mets played their baseball games from 1964 until 2008.

Kyle heard the crowd cheering inside and he remembered how excited he'd been the first time his mother took him to a game when he was seven or eight years old.

Allaire turned away from Kyle. "Can you hear me?" she asked through his earpiece.

Kyle nodded. "Yup."

"How about you, Ayers?" she asked.

"Yes, Ms. Allaire," Young Ayers answered.

Kyle handed Allaire a ticket, and held one himself. "Ready?"

Allaire nodded. She looked at the tracker screen. There were now three dots. Kyle had been right again. Ayers's red dot had reappeared as he and Sillow rode the 7-Train to Shea Stadium. Allaire had placed trackers on herself and Kyle now as well, so Young Ayers could help lead them in the right direction from his spot in the parking lot.

"We'll meet you right back here, Ayers, unless we tell you something different through your ear piece," Kyle said.

"Can I please come inside?" Young Ayers asked. "I bet I can help. I've never seen a baseball game."

"We need you to stay with the tracker, buddy," Kyle answered.

"But—" Ayers started.

Allaire walked up to him, and bent down to his eye level. "Kid, your fucking head will explode if you see him. You remember that?"

Kyle rolled his eyes at Allaire. "Real delicate way to put it."

Ayers cut in, "I know about my head exploding, but I still—"

"We'll see you in a little while," Kyle said. "Keep in your earpiece, and let us know if you see anything strange out here."

Kyle and Allaire headed toward Shea Stadium's Gate C. "This is the only baseball stadium I've ever been to," Kyle said. "It doesn't even exist anymore."

"I never got into sports," Allaire said. "No one ever taught me, so it just didn't hold that excitement for me."

When they got inside, they walked up the ramp toward the mezzanine deck and moved through the walkway. "Talk to us Ayers," Kyle said, peeking into one of the tunnels leading to the seats. "Are we moving toward him, or away?"

"It looks like you just passed him," Young Ayers said. "He was going in the other direction."

Kyle and Allaire turned around and started moving in the other direction. "They could've ditched the hats," Allaire said. They looked at each person's face as they passed.

"Now you're behind them," Young Ayers said, through their earpieces. "At least that's how it looks . . . But, Mr. Kyle, is the stadium all one level?"

"Of course not, Ayers," Kyle said, suddenly self-conscious that he looked like he was talking to himself. There would be a time soon when people would shamelessly walk around on their telephone all of the time, but they hadn't reached that point in 1997. "Come on," Kyle said, starting to jog, but still looking at faces as he passed them.

They jogged until they reached a set of ramps going up. Kyle and Allaire moved quickly toward the upper deck section and continued in the same direction moving away from home plate and into left field.

"You're getting closer," Young Ayers said.

They heard a roar suddenly as the crowd cheered for a Mets' run-scoring play.

They kept moving and reached the tunnel leading to section forty-four, some of the worst seats in the park—nosebleed level, and almost as far from the action as you could get.

"You're there," Young Ayers said. "Your three dots are very close together."

When they walked through the tunnel leading to the seats, they turned away from the field and saw that the entire section was empty, as were the two areas even further from the action, sections forty-six and forty-eight. Kyle squinted from the bright stadium lights not too far above them here in the upper deck.

Kyle turned and looked down over a railing at the field level seats. "They've got to be down there then," he said.

As they turned back toward the tunnel, something caught Kyle's eye. "Look."

"Where?" Allaire asked, missing it the first time.

Kyle pointed up to the furthest point in the ballpark to two specks in an entirely empty section—two heads barely visible above the backs of the chairs in front of them. Before Kyle could ask, Allaire had swung her backpack in front of her and was digging through. She handed him a pair of binoculars.

Kyle looked through and saw Ayers kneeling on the ground between two rows of seats, concentrating on something, while he and Sillow spoke. Kyle's heart sank when he saw his father nod at whatever Ayers was saying, and even smile a couple of times. He desperately wanted to think that there was no way Ayers could bring out a side of Sillow that Kyle wanted to believe didn't exist. But the truth was, they looked like buddies.

Allaire took the binoculars and looked herself while Kyle described the situation to Young Ayers. "Oh no," Allaire said, handing them back to Kyle.

Ayers was now sitting in a chair, and Kyle realized what he was putting together on the ground in front of him. "Shit. He's got a sniper rifle. It's got a silencer and everything."

"We need to get over there," Allaire said.

"If we try to stop him, he'll just shoot us, and still do whatever he was planning," Kyle said.

"Trying to assassinate a baseball team is exactly the kind of thing he'd do, just for fun," Allaire said.

As they moved out of the tunnel and back into the walkway, Allaire pulled two .45 caliber handguns from the waistband of her jeans, and handed one to Kyle.

"How did you get these past security?" Kyle asked.

Allaire raised her eyebrows. "If people ever start frisking girls, I've got big problems."

They started moving fast through the walkway toward section forty-eight when they heard a scream behind them. "Gun!"

Instinctively, Kyle and Allaire turned around

and saw a woman pointing at them. Four stadium police officers headed in their direction now, one of them frantically calling into his walkie for backup.

"Shit," Kyle said, raising his hands in the air as the cops headed toward them.

"What's happening?" Young Ayers asked through their earpieces. "Mr. Kyle? Ms. Allaire? What's going on?"

"I'll take the two on the left," Allaire said, putting her hands in the air as well.

"Hello? What's happening?" Young Ayers asked again, but Kyle and Allaire were too preoccupied to answer him. "Do you need my help? Is Ayers still up there with the sniper rifle?"

Kyle looked at her and shook his head. "Allaire, behave. We're not gonna hurt these cops."

"What should I do?" Young Ayers asked through the earpiece. Again, no answer. "Please, answer me . . . "

Before Kyle or Allaire could answer, though, they were being wrestled to the ground by all four cops. As the cops pulled them down, and took their guns and knives, Kyle tried to tell them about Ayers's sniper rifle. The cops were too jacked up with adrenaline, though, and just kept yelling, "Shut your fuckin' mouth," every time Kyle tried to speak. Both of them were pressed against the disgusting concrete of the Shea Stadium walkway and handcuffed. After being dragged up to their feet, the cops led them in the other direction down the walkway.

"There's a man with a sniper rifle in section forty-eight," Kyle said calmly. "What harm is there in checking out what I'm saying?"

"No one made it in here with a fuckin' sniper rifle," the shortest of the cops said. His nametag said "Sturgiano."

Allaire laughed. "We made it in here with guns."

"I'm glad you think this is funny," said the officer holding Allaire by her handcuffs. His name was Latavius, and he was chiseled. Without warning, he slapped Allaire hard in the back of the head. "Who's laughing now?"

"Hey!" Kyle yelled, pulling his hands away from the officer holding him. He moved toward Latavius.

"You want some too?" Latavius asked Kyle.

Kyle took a deep breath and tried to deflate his impulse to head butt the cop.

A short while later, they reached an elevator and the cops took them down to the Field Level section, through a series of doors labeled "Stadium Police." They pushed Kyle and Allaire into two hard plastic seats in a room with a desk and a couple of other cops doing paperwork.

For a little while, Kyle and Allaire took in their surroundings. Kyle was trying to figure out whether there was any chance they could escape, but it looked unlikely.

On a file cabinet, there was an old TV tuned to the ballgame going on right outside. The game was entering the fourth inning. All Kyle and Allaire could do was wait for whatever horrible outcome Ayers was planning.

"Ayers," Kyle whispered, hoping Young Ayers was still listening. "We're in the Stadium Police office on the lowest level."

"We have to do something," Allaire whispered, gesturing at their backpacks, sitting on the desk of one of the cops who brought them in. "Without our blots, we could wind up in jail here in 1997. It would be game over."

Kyle looked around the room. There were six cops, and he and Allaire were handcuffed, and without their weapons. He took a deep breath and pushed his back against his chair.

They heard the rumble of the crowd above them and Kyle assumed the Mets had scored again. But when he looked at the TV to see what had happened, the screen was dark. A few seconds later, the lights in the police office suddenly went out.

They heard the cops muttering to themselves,

in the pitch-black office. One of them opened the office door and confirmed that the entire stadium had lost electricity.

"We've never had a blackout here," a cop's voice said in the darkness. "Weird shit."

Allaire stood up, wondering if they could just walk out, but Kyle felt her get pushed right back down into the seat beside him.

"Don't you fucksticks try anything," a voice said. It sounded like Latavius, the one who'd smacked her.

CHAPTER 12

SEPTEMBER 29, 1997

a few minutes later

ONE BY ONE, THE POLICE OFFICERS LEFT THE room to help the crowd handle the sudden darkness. Each time the door opened, the tiniest bit of light flowed into the door of the office, which temporarily gave Kyle and Allaire back a sliver of vision for just a second.

They sat for more than ten minutes, now guarded only by one officer. If not for being handcuffed, it would've been an easy call.

"Now's the time," she said. "I need my bag."

The door flashed open and Officer Sturgiano walked back in, but sliding in right behind him, Kyle saw the outline of someone shorter and then he felt a tug on his arm. "Shh," a voice said near his ear. "Let's go." It was Young Ayers.

Kyle grabbed Allaire's arm and let Ayers lead them to the door.

"Wait," she whispered. "Backpacks and weapons."

"I'll get 'em," Young Ayers said. A few seconds later, he pushed Kyle and Allaire out the door of the Police Office and they were back out on the Field Level walkway, where the blue emergency lighting provided enough illumination to lead people out of the park.

Kyle noticed now that Young Ayers was wearing night vision glasses. He held all three of their backpacks, while Kyle and Allaire walked with their hands still cuffed behind them.

"Even with the blackout, we look a bit conspicuous here, guys," Kyle said.

"Open my bag, Ayers," Allaire said. "Small compartment. Should be the only thing in there."

Ayers did as she asked, and quickly pulled out

a handcuff key. He walked in back of Allaire, then Kyle, and set their hands free.

"What *don't* you have in that bag?" Kyle asked with a smile.

"How'd you kill all the lights in the entire stadium?" Allaire asked.

Young Ayers shrugged. Kyle could tell he was proud of himself. He'd come through for them. "I'll tell you, but you have to say it."

"Say what?" Allaire asked.

"That kids can kick some ass," Ayers said.

Allaire rolled her eyes, but smiled. "Kids can kick some ass . . . You happy? Now how'd you do it?"

"I went up to the entrance and started crying," Young Ayers said proudly. "I told a security guard my daddy was the guy who controlled the electricity for the whole stadium and he showed me to this one room . . . I stuck a gun in the guy's face and told him if he didn't kill all the lights in the stadium he'd never get to see his children again . . . But, there's one *more* way I kicked ass," Young Ayers said as they continued walking toward the exit. He gestured toward a man standing in the shadows behind one of the concession booths, right across from an exit to the parking lot. It was 18-year-old Sillow.

Kyle smiled and patted Young Ayers on the back. "How did you—?"

"It was so dark, I was able to grab him in all the commotion of the blackout without seeing Mr. Ayers," Young Ayers said.

"You could've been killed," Allaire said.

Sillow looked at Young Ayers with a look of recognition, but not Kyle. At this age, Sillow hadn't met the older version of his son, the time weaver, and likely hadn't even begun to contemplate having a child yet.

They walked over to Sillow and he looked at them with the same skepticism Kyle remembered from the first time he approached him at the hospital where he worked. "Are you all from the future too?" Sillow asked.

Kyle nodded his head noncommittally. "Kind of."

"That guy Ayers is a fucking maniac," Sillow said, turning his bandaged forearm toward them. "You see what he did to my arm? He took a piece of my bone out. Can you help me? Can you keep him away from me?"

"We'll get you home," Kyle said. "What year were you living in when you met Ayers?"

"Nineteen ninety," Sillow answered, which meant that this version of him was eighteen years old. "He tried to tell me we could live forever if I came with him. Said all this crazy shit."

"Come on," Kyle said. "We'll get you back home."

Allaire pulled out a silk blot and slid it over all four of them. Kyle wondered why the tunnel sounded like a construction zone lately, a repetitive clanging following them wherever they went. When they reached the rung for *1990*, Kyle pulled out a spare blot and stuck it inside the slot leading outside of the tunnel.

"Any chance you can forget all of this ever happened," Kyle asked, yelling over the noise in the tunnel, "and just live your life the same way you would have?"

Sillow shrugged. "Don't know . . . "

"You might notice things about yourself now," Kyle said.

"What kinds of things?" Sillow asked. The scowl was never too far from his face.

"The thing he did to you," Kyle said. "With your arm . . . You may find that you don't get older like everyone else."

"Maybe," Allaire said. "We don't really know."

"What happens instead?" Sillow asked.

Kyle shrugged. "Nothing. You just don't ever get old."

"What the . . . ?" Sillow asked. Then he smiled. "That sounds like some bullshit. Something that crazy fuck would've said."

Allaire shook her head. "You're special, Sillow. You'll see."

Sillow winked at her. "I'll show *you* how special I can be anytime you want, baby."

"Gross," Allaire answered.

"Take care," Kyle said, putting his hand on his father's shoulder. "I'll be seeing you."

"What's your name?" Sillow asked.

Kyle looked at Allaire. He wanted to tell Sillow to be a better father. "Better that we don't share too much," Kyle said after a long pause.

"Oh, hey, he put this thing on my hand," Sillow said. "Told it would help keep me safe, but I don't believe that asshole for nothin'."

Allaire held her silk blot up to Sillow's hand, and moved her face closer. She used her nail to pull the temporal tracker from his hand.

"Guess this thing's out of play now," she said.

"How 'bout telling me who wins the Super Bowl in '91, at least?" Sillow asked.

Both Kyle and Allaire shrugged. Young Ayers was already on the move through the tunnel.

Kyle watched as Sillow disappeared through the silk blot, into the slot, and back to his life in 1990.

CHAPTER 13

DECEMBER 3 & 4, 2016

nineteen years later

THE EIGHTEEN-YEAR-OLD SILLOW THEY'D BID farewell to in the tunnel was someone that Kyle didn't know yet. Someone he wouldn't know until the first time he wove back through time to ask his father for help in stopping a bus crash.

The crash of Bus #17, which killed twelve children when it was run off Banditt Drawbridge, did not exist in this timestream. Instead, more than three hundred kids were killed in an explosion at Silverman High School caused by one of the children "saved" by Kyle's efforts, which finally did stop the crash.

Kyle's father, Sillow, was one of the few people who knew about what was now the crash that never happened, and was partially responsible for stopping it. Kyle had sought him out for help in 1998, and then Sillow had come through in 2014 on the original day of the crash. Sillow was actually the one who drove the bus and dropped the twelve children back in downtown Flemming as the clock turned to midnight on March 14, 2014. He went back to his life in Florida right afterward, with his new wife and two young girls, and had only spoken with Kyle a few times since.

Kyle didn't know how Sillow would respond when he emailed four vouchers for one-way plane tickets to New York. A few days after sending them, though, with a note about wanting to meet his half-siblings for the first time, Sillow and his family arrived at the factory.

They came with two taxis full of luggage and looked like they'd planned to stay for a while, which was, of course, Kyle's hope. Before they'd even been properly introduced to Kyle and Allaire, eight-year-old Tinsley and ten-year-old Larkin were engaged in some type of game with Young Ayers that looked like tag. The sound of children's laughter in the factory was something new.

Kyle was surprised to learn that Sillow's wife, Yolanda, was an intellectual—an author and former professor of women's studies. Not exactly the match he'd have pictured for his father, but Kyle was glad to be surprised in this case.

At first Kyle had been shocked that Sillow could so easily pick up his entire family's life and move from Florida to New York, but the timing had actually seemed to work out perfectly. Sillow and Yolanda's house had been badly damaged in a recent hurricane, and they'd been living out of suitcases in a hotel. Sillow had also been recently laid off from his job at Jacksonville Central Hospital. It turned out they were actually eager for a change, and Kyle's email was the perfect catalyst.

The morning after they arrived, Kyle would be the one to deliver a surprise, as he and Sillow strolled down 7th Avenue on their way back to the factory from a trip to Starbucks. Kyle explained everything he knew about the Seres to Sillow. After dancing around it for a while, Kyle told Sillow that they were a part of this ancient bloodline. He explained how, technically, Sillow was a "second son," but that Ayers had proven far too dangerous to be tasked with watching over the ancient secret of time weaving. And, of course, Kyle explained that they would always be at risk of grave danger until they could find a way to subdue Ayers. And finally, based on the shortening of the tunnel, it was quite likely that Ayers's actions would lead to the end of the world if they couldn't figure out a way to stop him. Although this was *quite* a story, Sillow seemed to believe every word of it.

What Kyle proposed was simple: that Sillow and his family move into the factory, and take on the role that Yalé had before his death. Sillow would learn how to spin a silk blot, while Kyle and Allaire would continue to try to stop Ayers and limit the damage he did to the timestream. Together, Kyle told him, they would do their best to ensure that the universe continued.

"I want to say 'yes,' son," Sillow told him on their walk. "But I'm afraid I'll let you down."

Kyle smiled. "We're all in the same position. This is new to me too, because we had no idea you were a Sere."

Sillow shrugged at him. "It's a lot of responsibility, based on what you're sayin'."

"You showed up when I needed you," Kyle said. "And you just showed up again. I think the Sillow that used to let me down is in some other version of history . . . Like the bus crash."

Later that day, Allaire gave Kyle and Sillow the grand tour of the factory—the living quarters, the different machines for making silk blots, and she even opened up the huge cylinder which ran through the middle of every floor in the building. Allaire used an oven mitt and opened up a small hatch, letting Kyle and Sillow each peek inside at a huge dense forest of mulberry bushes, growing up from the bottom of the building. There were millions of silkworms and silkworm cocoons running through the huge cylindrical area.

"This living habitat provides all the silkworms you need," Allaire said. "There are instructions for the machines in Yalé's office . . . I mean, your office, Sillow. Some of them are written in Serican, but the pictures should help."

"Serican?" Sillow asked.

Allaire smiled. "It's the language of your people, but I'm afraid Yalé was the last person on the planet who could read or write it."

Sillow smiled. "Is there a book that can teach me? If I'm gonna do this, I want to learn it." Kyle knew Sillow had never even had an inkling about his own genealogy. Sillow's adoptive mother dying when he was nine led to him spending the rest of his childhood in foster homes and orphanages.

In the evenings, everyone in the factory slept on mats in the gym where Allaire used to train with Demetrius. While Kyle and Allaire didn't see a reason for Ayers to risk coming back to the factory building, they didn't want to risk the lives of the three children now living there in the event they were wrong, so they all slept in the same place and, more or less, took turns keeping watch.

One morning, Kyle opened his eyes and saw Allaire sitting cross-legged on the mat right next to his face. She was gently rocking back and forth and Kyle noticed tears in her eyes.

"What's going on?" he asked.

"It's gone," she said. "Ayers. The Silo. The pillars. Everything."

Kyle sat up and saw that they were the only two who were awake. "Gone how? The Silo doesn't even exist yet." He put his hand on her back and noticed her shirt was completely saturated with sweat.

She shook her head and blotted at her eyes with her wrists. "I dropped the retriever ball and the tunnel sounded short, but I had to see for myself. 2054 is the last year we can get to now. This is *it*, Kyle. If we don't stop this soon, there's going to be no 'us' anymore. Our world is going to be completely gone, along with everyone in it."

Kyle looked through the room at his new family. He didn't know his half-sisters well yet, and wasn't sure what he and Allaire were going to do with Young Ayers. But, he wanted them all to have a shot at a life together. With Ayers running around, rebelling against time itself, there was no telling how little they all had left.

"You having any more visions?" Allaire asked him. "Maybe visions about how to fix all of this? Because I don't feel like we have chance."

"We've got to find him again," Kyle said. "We just need to figure out a time and place we know he went. It's no different than before we ever had the tracker on him, or before I ever had that vision, right?"

"Your instincts have gotten better and better," Allaire said. "Do you think if we find him we're even going to have a shot?"

Kyle smiled. "How could I possibly know that?"

"You know a lot, Kyle Cash. Listen to your gut . . . Is it possible kill him?" Allaire asked again.

"Okay . . . " Kyle said, closing his eyes. For the first time, he tried to just listen to his own mind. It didn't sound any different to him. This wasn't like a certain year just flashing before his eyes. Until . . . he saw Young Ayers, headless, laying in a pool of blood and body parts. The image disturbed Kyle enough to jar his eyes open.

"Well?" Allaire said.

"I don't know, Allaire," Kyle said. "If we *can't* kill him, is there a room here where we can safely lock him up?"

Allaire nodded. "There's a cell Rickard built

down on the fourth floor. Rickard was your uncle, I guess. Not a good guy. If he hadn't died, I might've wound up in that cell myself."

"I'm not getting any kind of sense of where he is, or in what year," Kyle said. "Let's get online and start looking through major news events that are new to this timestream. Maybe we'll find a time and place where we can grab him."

Allaire looked as if she was about to throw up for a moment.

"What's wrong?" Kyle asked. "You sick?"

"I'm fine," she said, before standing up and heading out toward the restroom.

CHAPTER 14

DECEMBER 6, 2016

later that day

SINCE SILLOW AND HIS FAMILY ARRIVED AT THE factory, the three children had become fast friends. Young Ayers was so thrilled to have two playmates, it didn't matter to him that everything they played together was completely new to him. He'd read about games like hide and seek, and seen it on TV, but had never had a friend to play it with. And Tinsley and Larkin seemed to enjoy how provincial the older boy was, teaching him the "rules" to everything from soccer to playing princesses.

Still at square one in their search for Ayers, Kyle and Allaire tried to enjoy the time getting to know their new extended family. Living under the same roof as Sillow for the first time was strange for Kyle, who hadn't had the benefit of getting to know his father's day-to-day habits and quirks while he was growing up. He and Sillow had caught up on a lot of the big stuff during their efforts to stop the bus crash, but they hadn't yet developed a rapport suited for downtime or non-crisis moments.

Kyle walked into the kitchen of the factory and saw Sillow and Young Ayers sitting at a table together. "Hey, guys," Kyle said.

"Morning," Sillow answered. "Not sure if you're a meat guy, but I just made some bacon . . . Yolanda ran out and got some groceries. Those energy bars you got in those cabinets taste like sawdust."

Kyle grabbed a piece of bacon out of the pan and ate it. "This might be the best thing I've ever eaten," he said with a laugh. It had been a long while since he'd enjoyed something home cooked.

Young Ayers stood up without saying a word and left the room.

Kyle looked at his father. "What's that all about?

First time all week I've seen him without a smile on his face."

"He was asking me all about the other Ayers," Sillow said. "He's a good kid. You can tell just by spending five seconds with him."

"I'm hoping that, maybe, knowing what the other Ayers is doing and seeing him hurt people will be enough to change his destiny," Kyle said.

Sillow nodded. "Gotta be careful, though, son. He's just a young kid. He told me he knows what you and Allaire are looking for on that computer all day . . . Asked me if I thought Ayers was a terrorist. Also asked me if he was really safe here."

Kyle grabbed another slice of bacon and sat down, exhaling as he did. "Truth is, I don't know the answer to that . . . If we just let him grow up and ignore what he could become, then we risk there being two of these horrible monsters in the world."

"So, what, you'd just kill him?" Sillow asked.

"Probably not," Kyle said. "We're not even sure

we could. None of us really understands what nevering means, and whether the older Ayers doing it means the younger Ayers can't be killed either . . . We may reach a point where we need to lock the kid up for everyone's safety."

Sillow shook his head and exhaled. "You got it wrong, son, if you think locking him up is a kinder thing to do than killing him." Kyle hadn't thought of it that way before.

Allaire walked into the kitchen, and Kyle pointed to the bacon. "Try that," he said. "It tastes like a lazy Sunday morning."

She walked over to the pan and picked up a piece, sniffed it and put it back.

"How could you pass up bacon?" Kyle asked.

"Not hungry, I guess," Allaire said, scrunching up her face. "Come. I want to show you guys something."

Kyle and Sillow followed Allaire into the office right off the main factory floor. She sat down at the computer and opened up a window on the screen, calling up a *San Francisco Chronicle* article from a year earlier. "I couldn't find anything that seemed like it had Ayers's fingerprints on it," she said, "until I stumbled on this piece talking about how Halloween celebrations around the country were more subdued this year, and how crowds were so small in some places that the events were cancelled."

Young Ayers walked into the doorway and Kyle considered asking him to leave. But knowing that he was stressed about his place in their growing family unit, he didn't say anything.

Allaire clicked around with her mouse, moving too quickly for Kyle to read it. "So, I did some digging and found this thing that happened last year. These four gunmen, all in different costumes, just strafed the crowd with bullets at the big Halloween parade in the Castro neighborhood in San Francisco."

She zoomed in on the only picture they had of one of the shooters. It was impossible to know if it was Ayers underneath the soft rubber Justin Bieber mask, but it was certainly someone with similar murderous intentions. "The article says the four shooters just disappeared into thin air, slipping away even though a perimeter was set up around the entire area."

"How many dead?" Sillow asked.

Kyle couldn't help but look at Young Ayers, who seemed like he was trying to do his best to act unfazed, but was doing a terrible job of it.

"One hundred twenty-seven," Allaire said.

Young Ayers backed a few feet away from the doorway slowly, pulling his Rubik's Cube out of the pocket of his hooded sweatshirt. He stood in the hallway, head down, leaning against the wall and working on the puzzle.

"What are we waiting for?" Kyle asked. "Let's go stop this."

"We can't go back to stop the shootings," Allaire said. "But, if it's Ayers, we can try to grab him, cuff him and get him into a silk blot."

Kyle nodded. "Okay," he said, with less conviction than he wished he had. Even with his new role as the protector of time weaving, Kyle didn't know whether he could ever go back to a tragic event without having any inclination to change it. *Would it really be so bad if we grabbed Ayers before he started shooting?* he wondered to himself, knowing that he shouldn't be thinking that way anymore.

"I'm going with you," Young Ayers said, not taking his eyes away from his Rubik's Cube.

Kyle and Allaire looked at each other. It was a race to say "no."

"Sorry, kid," Kyle said. "It's way too dangerous. Remember? Your head could explode?" Kyle thought back to the vision he had earlier and again, he saw a clear image of Young Ayers's body, missing its head, laying in a bloody heap on the sidewalk.

"I have to see it for myself," Young Ayers said. "If he and I aren't the same person, I need to see *how* we're different."

Allaire turned to him. “You don’t have to come to prove that to us.”

“I have to prove it to myself,” he said, crying now. In some ways, the boy seemed so much older than twelve to Kyle. But he was just a child, and this all had to be very overwhelming.

Again, Kyle and Allaire looked at each other. Having an extra person there wouldn’t hurt. But, trying to make sure he stayed far enough away from the older Ayers to avoid any problems would be an additional concern.

Allaire shrugged, gesturing toward Kyle that it was his call.

“I, uh, I guess,” Kyle said. “But you’re going to need to stay as far away as possible, so you don’t get close to the other Ayers. Kyle wondered whether Young Ayers was thinking rationally enough at this point for it to make sense to bring him. He seemed very rattled to learn about a massacre that “he” may have caused.

CHAPTER 15

OCTOBER 30, 2015

thirteen months earlier

For all of the time weaving he'd done, it was Kyle's first time on an airplane, and the entire process made him nervous. Ever since they'd taken off, he'd been jumpy. Young Ayers was reveling in it, though, enjoying every second of his first flight. They'd let him pick out a bunch of candy from the Hudson News at JFK to take on the plane for the six-hour flight to San Francisco.

They'd gone through their silk blots to 2015, but after entering and exiting their blots in New York, they had to fly to San Francisco for the Castro neighborhood's Halloween festival where, tomorrow night, they believed Ayers and three other gunman would fire hundreds of bullets into a huge crowd of people.

Kyle marveled at how much time Young Ayers could devote to practicing the Rubik's Cube. Whereas Kyle would've thought that solving it once would be enough to make someone put it aside to pursue a new challenge, Ayers wanted to be the best. He wanted to get faster at solving it. And, he *was* fast. Kyle had been watching him for most of the flight and still didn't have the faintest idea as to how to solve it.

Allaire enjoyed the downtime on the plane, immersing herself in the lives of the stars through *US Weekly*, *People* and *In Touch* magazines, while Kyle sat in the middle seat, mindlessly gazing at the tiny TV in front of him and gripping the armrests every time they hit a small bump.

After one such bump, Allaire looked up from an article about the Kardashians and caught Kyle tensing up over a bit of turbulence. Kyle felt like his stomach was going to digest itself.

"You need to chill," she said to him, putting her hand on top of his.

Kyle shook his head. He was having trouble staying rational. "I just feel like—"

"This is safer than getting in a car," Allaire said. "In a car, you have the illusion of control, which makes it feel better, but it's actually much less safe."

Kyle white-knuckled the armrests for the rest of the flight, and felt a surge of relief when the pilot announced their final descent into San Francisco International Airport.

Allaire had long since given up on getting him to relax, but pulled him close by his shirt collar after the announcement and gave him a quick, hard kiss. "Told you everything would be fine."

About three minutes later, as the plane descended, there was a bigger bump than any of the others, and Kyle could feel the air shift the plane from pitching all the way to the left to all the way to the right. Kyle looked at Allaire and noticed that, while she didn't look overly worried, she *had* bothered to pick her head up from her magazine this time to look around. Kyle nervously looked up at the flight attendants, already strapped into their jump seats, and saw that they weren't alarmed either.

But then, a minute later, with the plane about ten thousand feet in the air—according to the flight tracker on Kyle's mini-screen—he heard a loud pop come from outside the plane. Now, when Kyle looked at the flight attendants, he could see them conferring with each other, concerned faces all around.

"Folks, from the flight deck," the pilot said over the loudspeaker a few seconds later. "Looks like we are having some mechanical difficulties. Shouldn't be a big deal, but just in case, we're going to ask that everyone take a brace position for the remainder of the flight while we do absolutely everything we can to try to bring the plane in safely."

That was enough to send the entire plane into a panic, and confirmed everything Kyle had been worrying about for the past six hours. He looked at Allaire, who was looking up toward the overhead compartment where they'd stored their backpacks.

One of the flight attendants did an admirable job of sounding calmer than she surely was as she reminded the passengers of how to take the brace position and prepare for impact.

As everyone on the plane was buckling in and panicking, Allaire stood up and grabbed their packs out of the overhead bin, tossing one to Ayers and one to Kyle.

"Ma'am," a flight attendant called out. "Take your seat and get into the brace position! You heard the pilot."

Allaire got back into her seat just before a huge bump, and then a quick drop of several thousand feet, which would've thrown her through the cabin. Allaire opened her pack and pulled out a silk blot. "Grab a blot," she said to Kyle and Ayers.

Young Ayers's face was blank. He had stopped playing with his Rubik's Cube, but now looked almost catatonic.

"Hey!" Allaire called to him, reaching over Kyle to grab his upper arm. "Get a silk blot out of your bag."

Without saying a word, Young Ayers pulled out a silk blot, and Kyle did the same.

"If we're going to crash, we need to get into the blot at the last possible moment," Allaire said. Because the second we leave the tunnel again, we're going to come out in the same geographical place. You don't want to freefall from a few thousand feet."

Allaire leaned over Kyle and looked out the window. The plane was descending very quickly, but the engines were still roaring, signaling that the plane was not in a freefall situation.

"If this doesn't work," Kyle said, "I just want you to know—"

"No!" Allaire said. "Not an option. Either these pilots are landing this plane, or we're bailing."

The screen in front of Kyle said they were now only a thousand feet off the ground.

"It's going to be quick," Allaire said. "If they don't announce that they've got this covered, we need to look out the window and pull the blots over us right before impact."

Kyle leaned over Ayers, who still hadn't said a word since the announcement from the pilot, and looked out the window. "Did you hear her, kid?" The ground was coming up quick, but Kyle could see the airport now.

"The landing doesn't look bad," Allaire said. "What do you think?"

Kyle shrugged. He'd never flown and had no idea how the landing was supposed to look.

The flight tracker on the screen said they were three hundred feet above the ground now.

Kyle watched as it went to two hundred fifty feet, then two hundred. He looked at Allaire, who looked out the window. He could tell she was as undecided as he was, even though she'd flown before.

"If we bail, and we time it wrong," she said, "we've got problems."

Kyle gave one more look at the flight attendants in their jump seats up at the front of the plane. They were looking out the small circular hole in the door of the plane. Kyle saw one of them whisper to another, and then they both smiled. People who thought they were seconds from dying didn't make jokes, Kyle thought to himself.

"Let's stay," Kyle said, his voice quivering with nervousness. "The landing's going to be okay."

Less than ten seconds later, the plane touched down on the runway to rousing applause from the relieved group of passengers.

"Thank you for bearing with us there, folks," the pilot announced. "And thank you for flying Continental Airlines today."

CHAPTER 16

OCTOBER 31, 2015

the next day

TRYING TO PUSH THROUGH THE CRUSH OF people at the Halloween celebration in San Francisco's Castro neighborhood was futile. The entire crowd moved—more or less—like some multi-celled organism, flowing one way, then the next. To try to buck the flow of people and go in your own direction was nearly impossible.

Kyle, Allaire, and Young Ayers were slowly moving toward the stage at the intersection of Castro and Market, where a faux-hawked lead singer screamed a song complaining about the oppressive popular music industry.

"We want to be behind the stage," Kyle screamed

toward Allaire's ear. "No one behind the stage was hurt in the shooting. We can sneak up on Ayers and grab him from there.

"Remember," she answered. "We have to let the whole incident happen. Remember this bus crash . . . Anything we do to try to save lives here could result in something worse down the road."

Kyle nodded. "I know." He knew she might be right, but he didn't know how he was going to watch more than a hundred people get murdered and not try to stop it. He could handle the thought of being the keeper of time travel, and of making sure the tunnel stayed clear of people trying to change the past. But this wasn't that. They were here for a reason, and they could either watch people die, or try to intervene as soon as they spotted Ayers and the other shooters.

Young Ayers stopped for a second to pick up a zombie mask he saw on the ground. It was a cheap, plastic number that didn't even have holes for eyes. No wonder someone had ditched it.

From the press coverage they'd seen, the shootings happened just before ten a.m., so they were only a few minutes away.

Kyle leaned down to Ayers. "Once we get there, you're going to see if you can crawl underneath the stage to stay out of the way. I know you want to help, but it's for your own safety."

Ayers looked hurt. "Then why did I even come?"

He was so mature that Kyle forgot sometimes that they were dealing with a child. He'd come along *because he had asked to*, but Kyle knew that wouldn't be a good enough answer. "I just need you to stay safe, and that's the best place for you."

They'd reluctantly gotten Young Ayers to climb beneath the wooden stage, while Kyle and Allaire knelt behind the stage, their heads peeking out, but their bodies concealed from view. It wasn't five minutes after they'd taken their places that the singer stopped in the middle of a song, and called out, "Get off the stage, you fuckin' jabronies."

Kyle craned his neck and saw that four guys had

jumped up on stage. From his clothing—the same gray shirt, vest, and jeans he wore the last time he saw him—Kyle could tell that the one wearing the big, rubber Justin Bieber mask was, in fact, Ayers. The other three wore masks too: a Bart Simpson mask on a guy with a three-piece suit; a Spider-Man mask on a cohort of Ayers's wearing long, flowing robes, and finally, someone in a full gorilla suit. None of them were holding guns.

"What the hell, guys?" the lead singer whined. "Get off the damn stage."

A few baffled security guys hopped up on stage and tried to lead the four intruders off, but the guys in masks brushed their arms away, and walked around the stage as if they were going to take over the music duties.

Then, the singer walked up to the guy in the Bart Simpson mask and tried gently pushing him in the chest toward the stairs leading off the stage. "C'mon, man. You're fuckin' up the show."

As soon as he did, though, Bart Simpson theatrically looked at the crowd and shook his huge head. The crowd let out some nervous laughter before Bart grabbed the singer's neck with one hand and held him by the throat for a second. Before security could even react, the masked man put one hand on each of the singer's cheeks and twisted his head, snapping his neck. The crowd let out a gasp, as Bart Simpson tossed the lead singer to the concrete beneath the stage. Ayers walked to an equipment box next to the drum kit as the rest of the band hurried to vacate the stage.

One by one, Ayers pulled machine guns out of the box and handed them to each member of his group. Before most people could comprehend what was happening, the four of them stood on stage with the guns as the crowd quickly began to disperse. But there was nowhere to go. As the pushing crowd from the stage area tried to escape, they came up against the wall of people stretching in every direction down the street.

Then, as Kyle heard sirens coming from beyond

the crowd, the gorilla suit guy started shooting into the crowd. As people ran, Kyle watched bodies fall to the ground, some shot, and some unlucky enough to be pushed and likely trampled. It was mass chaos.

The scene in front of Kyle and Allaire looked like something out of a war movie, as Ayers, in his Bieber mask, and his followers wearing the gorilla suit and the Spider-Man mask, joined in on the shooting too.

"I know we're not supposed to stop it, but I can't watch these people be executed," Kyle said, as he saw a young woman in a tiger print leotard get cut down with a shot to the back. She fell to the ground and stopped moving within seconds.

Kyle started to vault himself up to the stage, but Allaire pulled the back of his sweatshirt. "No!" she said. Then she turned to Young Ayers, who had popped out from his hiding spot when the shooting started. "You need to get back underneath the stage. Now!" She turned to Kyle. "I can't watch this happen either. Let's go."

Young Ayers didn't move. Every second they waited, more people would die. Ayers and his cohorts were shooting completely indiscriminately into the crowd, stopping only to reload.

"It's not a choice, Ayers," Allaire said. "Get under the stage. Now!"

"We'll tell you if we need you," Kyle said. "Go!"

Allaire and Kyle each held a .45, pulled from their backpacks. As the shooters moved across the stage, facing the crowd in front of them, Kyle and Allaire lined up clear shots from behind them.

"On three," Kyle said. "You take out the gorilla, and I'll get Bart."

"As soon as we do this, they're gonna turn and the gunfire's coming our way," she said.

"One," Kyle began. "Two. Three."

Kyle began shooting at the guy in the Bart Simpson mask. After a couple of misses, he hit him in the shoulder, which knocked him forward. He dropped his gun to grab at the bullet wound. Bart pulled off his mask to reveal a guy with a nineties flattop haircut. He looked around desperately trying to see where the shot had come from.

Allaire kept shooting at the gorilla while she knelt behind the stage, trying to keep out of view. But the gorilla absorbed the hits as if they weren't penetrating the suit. "He won't go down. He must be wearing a vest."

Kyle looked at how focused Allaire was on stopping the massacre in front of her. A short time ago, there was no way she'd have been willing to intervene. He knew she'd gone against all of her old ways, by trying to stop the bloodshed in front of her. But, watching her try to take down the gorilla erased Kyle's doubts about whether he could be a new kind of Seres leader: someone who didn't compromise human decency while protecting their great ability to time weave.

Kyle noticed six police officers running toward

the stage with their guns drawn. "Get down!" he screamed, pulling Allaire completely underneath the stage just as the crossfire between the police and Ayers's crew started. Kyle and Allaire joined Young Ayers who was huddled with his knees to his chest. Kyle could see that he was crying.

There was at least three minutes of back and forth bursts of gunfire between Ayers's shooters and the police. Above them, Kyle heard three distinct thuds and he wondered if the gunfight might be over.

Then, the shooting began again, and Kyle imagined the shock the police officers must've felt as they tried to take down Ayers and he simply didn't budge.

"We need to get him out of there before he slips away," Kyle said.

"Gotta wait for the shooting to stop, love," Allaire said. "I'm not letting you get killed today." Ayers sobbed, and Allaire put her hand on his knee. "It's okay, Ayers,"

He shook his head, and moved into a crouch. "I'm scared."

"Listen," Kyle said, raising his voice over the sound of the gunfire. "You're *not* him. I've spent enough time with you to know. The person out there is not you . . . *You* have compassion . . . Whatever he did to you—I know it was horrible—but you *aren't* him. You're a Sere, Ayers, and I need you."

Young Ayers nodded his head, and moved a little closer to the edge of their space under the stage. Any further and he'd be outside of the protected area where they were huddled together. The gunfire continued outside. "I'm so scared."

"Just be brave," Allaire said. "That guy out there may be the same in a lot of ways, but he is not *your* future. Kyle and I both see it."

"I'm so scared," he said once more. Then, after a lull in the gunfire for a few seconds, Young Ayers put on the zombie mask he'd picked up from the ground and scurried out from under the stage.

"Wait," Kyle called out, trying unsuccessfully to grab him.

"Don't worry," Young Ayers said through his tears. "The gunfire can't hurt me." He took his backpack off and handed it to Allaire.

"What are you doing?" Allaire said. "You can't go out there!"

"Remember what I told you," Young Ayers said. "Kids can kick some ass too." Then, Young Ayers just popped out from under the stage and was gone.

The gunfire started again, but Kyle and Allaire couldn't resist leaving the safe space under the stage to see where Young Ayers was going. They peeked above the level of the stage again and watched as Ayers continued to exchange gunfire with the police, who were now moving in, riddling him with bullets that had no effect. There were more police now too. Ayers had ditched the Bieber mask, likely to help his peripheral vision as he turned real life into a first-person shooter game.

Kyle and Allaire watched as Young Ayers calmly

walked onto the stage, holding the eyeless mask slightly away from his face so he could see the ground below his feet.

What had been a madhouse only minutes earlier was now a ghost town, except for emergency personnel tending to the wounded. More and more sirens filled the air from the growing contingent of ambulances and police cars.

Kyle cringed when he saw Young Ayers get hit by one stray gunshot, then another. The shots jarred him, but he kept moving, clearly having the same immunity to them now as the older Ayers, who still taking target practice at the police. The police must've been beyond baffled by now that no amount of bullets would take him down. The police gunfire stopped, though, and two officers raced toward the stage, likely to try to pull Young Ayers away from the firefight. Young Ayers sidestepped one cop, and ducked under the arm of another.

"They really *are* different," Kyle said to Allaire.

Before the cops could reach him, Young Ayers tapped older Ayers on the shoulder. Ayers turned around and looked at the boy, still wearing a mask over his face. When Young Ayers pulled the mask away, he stared right into the eyes of his older self. Simultaneously, they brought their hands to their heads, both clearly in immense pain.

"Oh no," Kyle said, resisting the urge to avert his eyes when he realized what was happening.

Allaire grabbed Kyle's hand, lacing her fingers into his.

Older Ayers dropped his machine gun to the floor as he let out a deep scream.

Kyle could see older Ayers's head slowly expanding, as if the bones underneath were stretching the skin. Young Ayers held his ears, grimacing, but his head didn't look to be feeling the effects yet. Kyle could tell he was trying hard to keep eye contact with his Older Ayers.

Older Ayers's face stretched on the growing skull beneath it. He looked at Young Ayers scornfully as the pain registered on both of their faces. "I protected you!" Older Ayers screamed, as he clutched the side of his head with his hands.

A few seconds later, Older Ayers's head exploded onto the stage, his unraveled brain rupturing violently into pieces and falling to the stage below. His body—minus his hands, which were blown off by the force of the blast—fell to the stage in a heap.

Kyle vaulted himself up onto the stage to grab Young Ayers, who stood there looking at the blood and brains in front of him, clearly in immense pain as he held his head as well. Kyle wondered: *Is there a chance to save him?*

"Ayers," he yelled, running toward him. Young Ayers shook his head violently as he saw Kyle running toward him. Kyle could see the fear in the boy's eyes. He wondered how long he'd planned to sacrifice himself.

Just as Kyle reached Young Ayers, he watched the kid's head do exactly what Kyle feared was inevitable. His head seemed to almost throb, as the inside became larger than the outside. The kid's brain exploded all over Kyle, splattering him with blood from head to toe.

Kyle fell to his knees and caught Young Ayers's headless body as it fell to the ground. He wondered if Young Ayers knew all along that this was the one way to kill someone who'd nevered, or if he was simply going on a hunch like Kyle and Allaire often were.

Of course, Kyle and Allaire had both seen this before, when Kyle's cellmate from prison, Ochoa, saw his younger self and his head exploded. Kyle thought about how little Ochoa—the sleeping baby in his mother's carriage—survived. Perhaps, Kyle thought, it was because the baby never actually saw his older self.

Kyle put his hand on Young Ayers's shoulder and began to cry. Although he'd done it again and again, his final act proved, once and for all, that he really wasn't the same as his monstrous, murderous older self. Would the selfless actions of this twelve year old allow Kyle and Allaire to save the world, Kyle wondered. Would they be able to extend this timestream and allow the human race to live past this generation? Or would the tunnel continue to shrink toward the inevitable end of humanity?

Kyle stopped sobbing when he felt the stage vibrating underneath him, which he quickly realized were footsteps coming up the stairs to the stage. He looked up and saw that he was surrounded by ten police officers, all with their guns drawn and pointed at him.

"Get up slowly," one of them said.

Kyle did not have a silk blot on him. The blots were in their backpacks, which were next to Allaire, who was still out of sight behind the stage. If he were somehow blamed for all of this, he wouldn't have a way to get out of jail.

"Hands on top of your head," another cop bellowed.

Kyle looked toward Allaire, but then quickly looked away, trying not to draw the attention of the officers to her.

When he didn't see her, though, he panicked. He wondered whether the police had grabbed her when he ran onto the stage. Kyle jumped when he heard an explosion come from behind them, up Market Street, in an area vacated by the scrum of people escaping the gunfire.

For a brief moment, the attention of all of the police officers was off of Kyle. He saw Allaire waving him over from the sidewalk next to the stage and he hustled away, sprinting as fast as his body would allow him.

By the time the police started moving toward him, Kyle was almost to Allaire. He felt a gunshot hit the ground right next to him, but by that point he was able to get one foot into the silk blot Allaire was holding out for him. She followed right behind him.

He was never so happy to see the inside of the

tunnel and he collapsed against the hard metal trying to catch his breath. Then, he thought about Young Ayers again and felt a hole in the pit of his stomach.

CHAPTER 17

APRIL 18, 2017

one-and-a-half years later

Kyle and Allaire climbed through the tunnel without saying much. They'd started the day as a threesome, and it felt extremely lonely without Young Ayers around. They'd spent so much time mistrusting him that Kyle hadn't realized how much he'd become part of the tenuous fabric of their lives in the time they'd spent together. Without many people to hold onto, Kyle couldn't help but feel connected to the few he could.

When they reached the rung labeled *2016*, Allaire pulled the silk blot toward the slot, but Kyle put his hand over hers. He shook his head.

"We can check on the tunnel later," she said.

"I just want to get back. You have blood all over you. You need a shower."

"Sillow needs time," Kyle said. "If we want him and his family to make the factory their home, we need to let them settle in without us. Let's go to 2017."

Allaire nodded and kept climbing through, ahead of Kyle.

"You're quiet," Kyle said, following closely behind Allaire.

"You should talk," she answered.

"I'm just rattled," Kyle said. "Losing the kid . . . And, now that the other Ayers is gone too, if the tunnel *doesn't* get longer again, I don't know what we're supposed to do."

"I don't know either," Allaire said. "But, we have to think positively. Ayers is dead! I don't even remember what it's like not to be chasing after him, or cleaning up one of his messes."

They'd achieved exactly what they wanted to in killing Ayers, but it happened in the worst way possible, by losing one of their own. There was still a part of Kyle—buried much deeper now than before—that felt that if anyone deserved misfortune, it was him.

"It's been a while since the timestream has been clear of obvious danger," Allaire said. "If we see the tunnel start to grow again, then we get to live our lives at the factory and just hope that everything stays quiet forever."

"Forever," Kyle said.

"'Til death do us part," Allaire answered, and for the first time Kyle thought about the idea that they could have a real, *almost* normal life together. He was the Sere heir now—there was no one left to say differently—and Allaire was the person he'd eventually marry. Not yet—in his natural timestream, he was still only eighteen years old—but sometime in the future.

No more threats. No more threads to clean up. Just a real future. He'd be a different kind of Sere heir than Yalé. And he'd be different from the other

Seres Allaire told him about. He would try to protect their great secret without cutting himself, or the rest of his family, off from the outside world.

"It's going to be different," Kyle said. He wanted her to know too that they were going to make a better life. He smiled, the fantasy of an endless tunnel an intoxicating thought.

Allaire stopped climbing through the tunnel and turned toward Kyle. She pulled him by his bloodstained shirt and kissed him in the way that drove him crazy. "Let's drive cross country back to New York," she said.

Kyle had never been anywhere. Even his time weaving had all taken place in New York. Other than a few trips with his mom, or a few class trips, all in the northeast, Kyle had spent his entire life inside New York State. "That's a great idea," he said. "But we should check the tunnel first. See if it's gotten longer."

"No," Allaire said, putting her finger on his lips. "Let's just go. We'll check the tunnel when we're back. I've spent my life in this tunnel, and it's time for a break."

He was anxious to start their new, more relaxed life together, and after a few more minutes of kissing, they both eagerly climbed toward 2017.

Three weeks later, Kyle and Allaire returned to the factory building in New York. Their drive across the country had been a revelation. It was the first time they'd spent time together without a crisis going on around them. They'd gotten some strange looks from hotel clerks and other guests during the course of the trip—although Allaire was a young looking thirty-five-year-old, when looking at the couple, there was no debating that she had at least a decade on Kyle, who still had a baby face at eighteen.

While it was Kyle's first trip beyond the northeast, it was the longest stretch of Allaire's life that she'd devoted to leisure. Her time with the Seres had been so solemn. Even before Ayers was born, which simultaneously gave her purpose and put her in danger, her life had been completely isolated from the outside world.

After their three-week trip, Kyle led Allaire off the elevator on the fifth floor of the factory. They both seemed to know right away that everything had changed. This was confirmed when they saw a chandelier hanging in the elevator bank. It was nothing fancy, but it provided more light than the area had ever had before.

They walked inside the main factory room and found all three machines running. Someone had built a fourth console in the room as well, which looked almost like a drying rack, with several silk blots hanging off of it.

Kyle heard the patter of footsteps coming toward them and saw Sillow's daughter, Tinsley, run into the room, skidding in her socks across the tile floor. "Hi Kyle," she said. "Hi Allaire!"

"You've gotten big, sweetie," Kyle said to his younger half-sister, who had aged a year-and-a-half since he'd last seen her. "Where is everybody else?"

"Mama's cooking dinner, and Daddy and Larkin are playing Monopoly," she answered, dancing across the room, twirling a few times for them. "I *hate* Monopoly."

Kyle started in the direction of the back area of the fifth floor, toward the kitchen and bedrooms.

He turned back and saw that Tinsley had grabbed Allaire's wrist, swinging her arm in front of her playfully. "When's cousin Ayers coming back?" Tinsley asked her.

Allaire gave the girl a toothless smile and looked at Kyle.

She gently pulled her wrist away. "I'm thinking we should get ice cream tonight, if your mom and dad say 'okay' . . . What do you think?"

Tinsley did a little ballet jump and shook her head "yes" before running off back down the hall, past Kyle.

The factory looked as if they'd brought in an interior decorator. Walls had been painted more inviting colors, comfortable furniture had replaced the industrial looking pieces that were there before.

As Kyle walked into the kitchen, he stopped and just looked around for a few minutes before even saying a word.

"It looks like a home," Allaire said to Sillow's wife, Yolanda.

Yolanda looked up from stirring a huge pot. "That's what I was going for . . . Thank you for saying that."

Kyle looked around. The entire room had been transformed. What used to be a barebones cooking range and refrigerator now looked like the kitchen in an expensive suburban home. "How did you—?"

"I'm used to working," Yolanda said. "I needed something to keep me busy here."

Allaire nodded and Kyle could see that she empathized. In order to live here long-term, things would need to be different. In addition to being less isolated, they'd need to be less utilitarian.

"It looks amazing," Allaire said. "Truly unbelievable."

"The girls are in school," Yolanda said. "At first, I bought into the home schooling, but New York's the greatest city in the world. I'm not going to have my girls live here and never even get to experience it."

Kyle wondered how Allaire felt hearing Yolanda's words. If Allaire had had someone advocating for her the same way, she would be a different person. She'd be someone who had experienced the world outside the factory's walls.

Yolanda put her cooking spoon down next to the fancy stove and wiped her hands on a dishtowel. "I hope it's not a problem for you that I put them in school."

"Of course not," Kyle said. "We'll just need to make sure the girls are careful once they're old enough to understand what we do here."

"They think we just moved into a funky new apartment," Yolanda said.

"Where's Sillow?" Kyle asked.

Yolanda smiled. "In his office . . . He's really embraced all of this . . . "

"Oh really?" Kyle asked with a slight smile. Bringing Sillow here had been his idea, but the reality was that he didn't know his father all that well. There'd been no guarantee that the experiment would work.

"Go see for yourself," Yolanda answered.

Kyle looked over at Allaire. "You coming?"

She smiled at him. "Go see your father . . . I want to see what smells so good." Allaire walked toward the stove.

"It's vegetable stew," Yolanda said. "We've got an organic garden up on the roof. Lots of stuff beginning to grow now that it's gotten warmer."

Kyle walked down the hall to the room he'd always known before as Yalé's office.

CHAPTER 18

APRIL 18, 2017

moments later

AGAIN, KYLE NOTICED THE OFFICE HAD BEEN transformed. When Yalé was alive, the room he worked in simply had a desk, chair and a file cabinet. Sillow's office had papers and blueprints pinned to the wall. They'd repainted it a dark blue, which made the room feel imposing, and Sillow had set himself up with a new computer—a high-end Mac with a huge monitor.

Sillow looked up from the floor where he sat cross-legged next to Larkin with a Monopoly board in front of them.

"Hello, son," Sillow said.

"Hi, Kyle," Larkin said, springing up to hug

him. Larkin had a head full of curly ringlets, which bounced when she moved. She ran into Kyle and squeezed his waist.

"Lark," Sillow said, standing up, "why don't you go help Mommy in the kitchen while your big brother and I catch up."

She nodded and started toward the door. "I'm happy you're back, Kyle." Larkin left and Kyle turned back to Sillow.

"They're doing well here, huh?" Kyle asked.

Sillow nodded.

"He's gone," Kyle said. "Ayers. The boy too."

"You did what you needed to," Sillow said.

Kyle shook his head. "No. The kid sacrificed himself. We wouldn't have gotten Ayers if he hadn't. He knew there was no choice, and that we wouldn't have let him do it. The kid's a hero. And it's so strange. The evil inside of Ayers could have ended the world, but the good inside of the boy . . . I don't know. It's confusing." Kyle pointed to the walls, changing the subject without speaking. He looked over at the different stacks of folders on Sillow's desk. "Looks like you really dove in."

Sillow smiled. "You have no idea, Kyle. This stuff is more fascinating than even just time travel."

"*Just* time travel?" Kyle said. "What more is there?"

"Time travel is the part you can see," Sillow said. "I'm trying to figure out the things we can't see . . . Yet."

"What kind of things, Sill . . . Dad?" Kyle asked.

Sillow walked up to a huge chart on the wall. It had large letters that were completely foreign to Kyle, with writing underneath. This looked like the same language that was etched into the wooden paddle Young Ayers had been swinging around just before they traveled to 2015.

Kyle followed Sillow over to the wall and stood next to him. "Their language—*our* language—it's all numeral based. The numbers just don't look like what we're used to. The different number combinations make up words, but just like in Spanish where words are male or female, the Sere language assigns a numerical value to each word. And, it usually kind of makes sense."

"I'm lost," Kyle said.

"There's no time to teach you the language now," Sillow said. "Not this minute, at least." He slid over to another huge paper hanging on the wall. This one was old, framed behind a piece of tall, thin glass. "But, look here at this . . . "

Kyle saw the same characters, but this time, they were stacked on top of each other. Sillow had post-it notes all over the frame. One said "inside-out." The other said "man-made." And another said "second son/second daughter."

"What *is* this?" Kyle asked.

"From what I can gather," Sillow said. "This is the most important thing in this entire factory. It explains how to create the machine to build a silk blot."

"But that machine's already been built," Kyle said.

"Yes," Sillow answered. "But, who wrote these instructions? And how did *they* figure it out? That's the exciting part."

Kyle nodded.

Sillow continued, "This comes from before there was even a tunnel, or maybe when the tunnel was very small."

"It says how the tunnel was built?" Kyle asked.

"Not really," Sillow answered. "It says that the tunnel is supposed to be built inside out, by someone called 'the rebel.' It took me forever, but there's really no other translation I can find that works. It's 'rebel.'

"What does 'inside out' mean? Who's the rebel?" Kyle asked.

Sillow smiled and shrugged. He walked over to another paper hanging on the wall. This one looked like a technical drawing of a circular space. "Recognize this?"

"It's not the tunnel," Kyle said.

"That's right," Sillow answered, leading Kyle out of the room. He pointed to the round cylinder that ran through each floor in the factory.

"That's where all of the worms are," Kyle answered.

"Yes," Sillow answered. "According to my papers, it's called the 'colony chamber.'"

Kyle followed Sillow back inside his office.

"So, what does any of this mean?" Kyle asked.

Sillow looked troubled for a second, and sat down in the chair behind his desk. Kyle sat across from him. "I don't think this whole thing—the tunnel, and time weaving . . . I don't think it was meant to go on forever. Everything I've read in these different papers seems to reference the tunnel being temporary . . . Yalé was trying to figure this stuff out too. I've got all of these old papers written in Serican, and they mention a second son repenting for some great sin. Like he'd done something wrong, and now was being punished. And it seems like, somehow, the tunnel is involved in the punishment. But, I haven't seen anything to make me think it was supposed to be this permanent thing that just stays there."

"But what happens when the tunnel goes away?" Kyle asked.

Sillow shook his head. "These papers are all very old, and they tend to repeat themselves a lot. We come from a long line of people with a lot of time on their hands. For every answer I've found, there's another question that comes up . . . Maybe, the tunnel goes away, and that's it. No more time weaving. Maybe, the tunnel is the way humanity keeps going and without it, there's nothing."

"So what do we do?" Kyle asked. "What do *you* think we should do?"

Sillow shrugged. "I think we need to check on the tunnel. If it's longer, or at least holding steady, we have some time to figure this all out."

"And what if it's still getting shorter and shorter?" Kyle asked.

Sillow smiled. "Then we're going to have to figure out what's on the other side."

"The *other side*?" Kyle asked.

"There's something out there," Sillow said. "Everything I've found here keeps using the words 'inside out' when it mentions the tunnel, but that's all it says. The tunnel doesn't exist here, but it exists *somewhere*. If it's going away, we need to figure out why and how to stop it, and the answer is beyond those walls."

Kyle smiled at the audacious suggestion. "You realize that the tunnel is made of steel, right? And the silk blots are too small to bring any big equipment inside."

Sillow opened the drawer to his desk and pulled out a huge drill with a bit thicker than Kyle's thumb. "Solid diamond bit. If anything can get through the walls of the tunnel, it's this . . . Diamond cost me nine grand. Good thing there's a few hundred g's in petty cash laying around here."

Kyle pressed the button on the drill and it came

to life. "You bought this so we could drill through the tunnel?"

"If it's cooperating, and not shrinking on us," Sillow said, "then we leave her alone. We wait and see . . . But if you get in there and it's shrinking, then how could you argue that it's time to break through?"

Yolanda appeared in the doorway. "Who's hungry?"

CHAPTER 19

APRIL 18, 2017

one hour later

IT WAS THE FIRST HOME-COOKED MEAL HE'D HAD in years. It was also the first real family meal Kyle had ever had. Sillow's daughters would grow up in this strange place, as part of this strange tradition, but it was alright, Kyle thought. The things Yolanda and Sillow had done to warm up the factory made it feel like an actual home.

Even in this room, the walls were still padded. But, with draperies and artwork hanging, you could barely notice that it was once a gymnasium. They'd turned it into a dining room so they could achieve the normalcy of family dinners together, and they'd succeeded. For the first time, the factory building didn't seem like such a dreary place to Kyle.

"You should check in on your mother now that you're back," Sillow said to Kyle.

Kyle nodded as he finished a bite of stew. His mother was the missing piece to this family meal, even if she didn't necessarily fit in amongst Sillow and his new family . . . Kyle would have to go see her on his own.

"Are we going to stay here now that Kyle is back?" Larkin asked Yolanda and Sillow.

"Of course we are," Yolanda answered, smiling warmly at Kyle. Then, he saw Yolanda's eyes get bigger and her attention shift to Kyle's right, where Allaire looked like she was trying to keep herself from throwing up.

Allaire bolted to the bathroom while everyone sat for a second looking at each other.

"She's gonna hurl," Tinsley said with a giggle, which made her sister laugh as well.

Yolanda stood up and took her napkin from her

lap, laying it on the table next to her bowl. "I'll check on her." She walked toward the bathroom and stood outside the door, speaking to Allaire, but Kyle couldn't hear what they were saying.

"She's had something with her stomach for a few days now," Kyle said to Sillow.

What Kyle didn't say, of course, was that he was concerned that what Allaire was feeling was somehow related to time weaving. Perhaps she was developing some condition as a result of so many trips through the tunnel. He thought about how they'd definitely changed the outcome of the shooting in San Francisco, saving lives, and certainly altering the timestream in the process. So far, they hadn't seen any repercussions and Kyle hoped that this wasn't one. He tried to think back to when Allaire first mentioned her stomach bothering her, but he couldn't recall. Kyle's amazing memory was now routinely counteracted by going back and forth through the timestream. Keeping track of exactly what events happened, and when, was nearly impossible for him these days. His photographic memory had been a casualty of time weaving.

A few minutes later, Yolanda walked back through the dining room holding her wallet. "I'm just going to run to Rite Aid for some ginger ale and Pepto. Allaire's gonna lay down . . . "

Kyle stood up from the table.

"Seriously, Kyle, sit . . . " Yolanda said. "Nothing to worry about. She's just going to rest. She wants you to finish your dinner."

Kyle tentatively sat down and nodded, polishing off the rest of his bowl of stew, and then going back for seconds, and even thirds.

Later that evening, Kyle joined Allaire in bed.

He was surprised when she turned toward him.

"I thought you were asleep," Kyle said. "Sorry if I woke you."

Allaire shook her head. "I can't sleep."

Kyle nodded. "The stuff Sillow was telling me, none of it makes perfect sense, but it's all so unbelievable. He thinks that there's something on the outside of the tunnel. He says if the tunnel is still shrinking that we need to break through it."

Allaire smiled at Kyle. He could tell her head was somewhere else.

"I'm sorry," he said. "I'm such a jerk . . . How are you feeling?"

Allaire nodded and smiled. Her eyes were full. Her face didn't make it look like she was crying, but her eyes did. "I'm alright."

"I'm glad," Kyle said.

"It's different here now, right?" Allaire said. "Don't you think?"

Kyle nodded. "I can't believe what they've done."

"Does it still feel like a sad place to you?" Allaire said.

"Allaire, what's going on?" Kyle asked.

Tears streamed from the corners of Allaire's eyes. "It doesn't feel like a sad place anymore, does it?"

Kyle shook his head. "No. I think it's the people that make a place feel sad or happy. But a fresh coat of paint doesn't hurt either . . . You're not thinking of leaving, are you?

"Of course not," Allaire said, wiping tears from her face. She moved closer to Kyle now, and grabbed his hand, interweaving her fingers with his. "My entire life's been here," she was finally able to say. "I grew up on this floor."

"You're so much more than this place, Allaire," Kyle said to her.

"Can I make somebody happy?" she asked. "What if I can't?"

Kyle brushed some hair out of her face. "You make me happy . . . What's going on? Where is this coming from?"

"Do I really make you happy?" she asked. "You know the darkness inside of me. You know the things I've done."

"We're more than our pasts, Allaire," Kyle said. "I'm done thinking about what I've been. Just because we've relived the past over and over doesn't make it more meaningful. The things I want aren't in the tunnel. I want the days in between. With you. *That's* what I want."

Kyle pulled her in tight and let her sob against his chest. He stroked her hair, and down the smooth length of her back. Having her in his arms felt more than right. It felt perfect. Everything he'd seen—everything he'd gone through to get to this moment—felt worth it to him right then. There was no one else who would ever belong in his arms like this. He put his lips on her forehead as she cried. He could feel the heat emanating from her sobbing breaths, but still pulled her closer. He had to resist the urge to squeeze her so hard it might hurt her.

She kissed him—little kisses, over and over—and looked him in the eyes. It was the most vulnerable he'd ever seen her. "Do you think a child can grow up happy here?" she whispered.

Kyle smiled at her, looking back at her as deeply as she was at him. "Tinsley and Larkin are going to be great here. We're a family now. We'll make this place everything it needs to be for them."

Allaire buried her head in Kyle's chest, and for a second he thought he'd upset her. "Not just them," she said. When she looked back up at him, she was smiling. It was a smile that barely fit between her cheeks.

"What?" Kyle asked, gently moving his hand to her shoulder.

All of a sudden, Allaire's crying had turned into a case of the giggles. She couldn't stop herself from laughing. It was one of the first times Kyle had ever seen her relax enough to be silly.

"What are you trying to tell me?" Kyle asked.

She took a deep breath and stopped laughing. She moved her face right up to his again and looked him in the eyes. "Yolanda got me a pregnancy test."

Kyle reached around her and pulled her closer again. "What?"

"You heard me, Kyle Cash," she answered.

"And?"

Her smile said it all for him.

Kyle kissed her. "Are you happy?"

She nodded, tears streaming from her face again. "So happy . . . But, are you?"

Kyle was only eighteen years old. The person he was before he ever traveled through a silk blot didn't know if he'd ever have children, much less soon. He'd wondered, even after he got out of prison, if anyone would ever want to have a family with someone who had killed twelve children. But, that was before Allaire. Before this beautiful woman. Before this person he'd grown with . . . When they met, Kyle was still a guilt-ridden boy in juvenile detention. And Allaire was still a hardened, violent woman.

Kyle was still eighteen, but he'd fallen in love with someone who, when they lived in the same timestream, was thirty-five. They weren't going to have this opportunity forever, and there was no doubt that he wanted any future that came, so long as Allaire was a part of it. He knew Allaire was going to be an amazing mother, and would pass along to their child all of the love she'd been deprived of.

"Of course I'm happy," he said. "Happier than I've ever been."

CHAPTER 20

APRIL 21, 2017

three days later

IT WAS AFTER THEIR FIRST DOCTOR'S APPOINTMENT together, when they got to listen to the baby's heartbeat, that Kyle and Allaire made the decision that she wouldn't go inside the tunnel again while she was pregnant. They were only one year off from their natural timestreams here in 2017, and it didn't make either of them comfortable to risk bringing the still developing baby inside the tunnel. Kyle and Allaire knew that they could handle the effects of time traveling, but they'd have no way to know how the fetus would respond. If the baby didn't have the genetic disposition to time weave, the consequences could be disastrous.

Later that afternoon, Kyle and Allaire were in Sillow's office, putting together Kyle's backpack for a trip into the tunnel. All he was planning to do was check whether the tunnel had shrunk or extended since the last time Allaire had measured, or whether it still went to 2054.

Sillow handed Kyle the drill with the diamond bit.

"We can't drill through the tunnel," Allaire said. "There's no way to know what would happen."

Sillow shrugged. "And, what happens if it shrinks past 2017? We don't know what happens then either . . . Do you want to take that risk?"

"I still don't think Kyle should go in there by himself and just start drilling," Allaire said.

Sillow pointed up at the wall of his office. "Everything I have here says the tunnel is supposed to be temporary. What if it's us? What if we're the ones who are supposed to break through? Doesn't this all feel like a new beginning to you?"

Allaire turned to Kyle. He could see the fear in

her eyes. "I know that he's done a lot of reading up," she said, pointing at the walls. "And this is impressive. But, you and I have been out there. We've seen how powerful all of this is. Whatever's controlling the tunnel is a lot stronger than we are."

Kyle dropped the drill into his bag alongside the red tracker ball and stopwatch. This had been Young Ayers's backpack on their last trip through the tunnel. The paddle with ancient Serican writing that Ayers had found in Yalé's office was still in the backpack as well. "You're both going to have to trust that I can make the right decision," Kyle said to her.

Kyle walked from Sillow's office to the main factory room and pulled a silk blot off of the rack. Sillow and Allaire followed behind him.

"Are you sure I shouldn't come too?" Sillow asked.

"Some of the old rules were dumb," Kyle said. "But keeping one adult Sere here at the factory at all times makes sense. I'm afraid I've got to do this myself, Dad."

"Please be careful," Allaire said. The look of fear in her eyes was new to Kyle. She wasn't someone with the temperament to sit on the sideline.

Sillow looked at the two of them and turned around, leaving the room.

"I'll be okay," Kyle said.

"I've never felt invested in the future before," Allaire said. "I've never really *cared* about the future. I want to meet our baby, Kyle. I want our child to grow up and have a life."

Kyle smiled at her. "*Our* child . . . will have a life."

"Then, you need to listen to me," she said. "If there's anything on the outside of that tunnel, it's bad. The tunnel has been around longer than you or me, or Sillow. Why would we take any huge risks?"

Kyle felt like he was talking to a different person, but in many ways, he was. Allaire was already a protective mother, even though their baby hadn't been born yet.

"I promise I'm not going take any unnecessary risks," Kyle said. "I want to make sure our baby is safe too . . . I love you."

Kyle kissed Allaire on the forehead and pulled her into his chest.

"Be careful," she said.

"I'll be right back," he answered. "I love you."

A few seconds later, Kyle ducked into a silk blot and was back inside the tunnel.

CHAPTER 21

APRIL 21, 2017

moments later

JUST AS THEY'D EXPERIENCED EARLIER, THE tunnel was louder than it used to be. Kyle tried to pinpoint where the *clang, clang, clang* was coming from, but it was hard to tell. It sounded as if it were coming from beyond the tunnel—somewhere outside of its walls. As curious as Kyle was about the question of what was beyond the tunnel, he agreed with Allaire that, right now, with a baby on the way, they needed to be protective of the status quo. They wanted their baby to have a life, and angering whomever was beyond the tunnel was not their best way of ensuring stability.

Kyle pulled the metallic red ball from his backpack. He pulled out his stopwatch, and pressed the button on the ball to ensure it would roll back to him. He tossed it into the tunnel, started the timer, and waited.

It was only a little while later that Kyle heard a ping. *It can't be*, he thought to himself. If the ball had really hit the end of the tunnel already, it would mean it had shrunk significantly.

When the ball rolled back to Kyle, he sent it through the tunnel again, and again, it timed out to only about ninety seconds, which, Kyle assumed, had to be some kind of mistake. *Perhaps there was something else in the tunnel blocking the way?* Kyle wondered.

Once the ball rolled back to him, Kyle dropped it into his backpack, along with the stopwatch, and started climbing through the tunnel in the direction of the future. Kyle couldn't let himself consider the idea that the tunnel had shrunk again. Ayers was dead, as was his young doppelganger. Kyle thought about what Yalé had said to him right before he killed himself. *Could I be the problem?* Kyle wondered. *What if the reason the tunnel is shrinking is because of me?*

He continued to climb through the tunnel, past the rung labeled *2018*. As he moved past *2018*, the clanging sound got even louder, and the air in the tunnel felt different. Kyle climbed through more quickly, moving from rung to rung as fast as his body would let him.

This was the first time Kyle had been alone since Allaire had told him they were going to have a baby. He considered the idea of bringing a baby into such an uncertain world. Other people were getting pregnant right now and had no idea of the tenuous goings-on within the timestream. But, Kyle was actually in a position to impact their fates, and his own. In that moment, he felt an intense pressure because of it.

Kyle began to feel like he was spinning. It suddenly became harder for him to breathe, and he had to stop moving. *What's happening?* he wondered.

He looked around him, but nothing had changed. The tunnel wasn't shaking like it had once before. Gravity was not pushing down on him. The more Kyle took shallow breaths, the better he felt and in a few minutes, he realized that it was old-fashioned panic he was feeling—a panic that had been completely self-induced. There was so much more at stake now, and Kyle's subconscious was onto that fact.

Just as he began feeling better, the spinning feeling started again. This time, he had a clear image in his head the entire time, as he tried catching his breath. He saw Allaire, holding a baby in the factory. Sillow and Yolanda were there. The two girls, too. Kyle searched the mental photograph for himself, but he wasn't there. *Where am I?* he wondered.

Once he'd gotten himself under control again, Kyle moved quickly to the rung for *2019*, and once he got there, he saw what he had feared. The end of the tunnel was right in front of him.

Twenty months, Kyle thought to himself. *Is that all the time the world has left?* He banged on the metal blocking his way with both fists. "What the hell?"

He opened the backpack and looked at the drill. He'd made Allaire a promise that he'd be cautious. But neither of them had imagined the tunnel shrinking this much. For all he knew, the tunnel could shrink again as soon as he went back to 2017, and Kyle, Allaire and their unborn child might just evaporate.

He pulled the drill out and decided to make a hole just large enough to look through. He pressed the drill's trigger and watched the diamond bit spin. He had his doubts that it would even work. He thought of all of the people in the world waiting to meet their unborn children. The fate of the universe felt different to Kyle than it had before. Something theoretical to him had become completely personal the moment he learned that Allaire was pregnant. The bit spun against the heavy metal of the tunnel, but had no effect.

Kyle held the drill in his hand and pointed it at the wall in front of him again. He touched the wall once, then held the drill against it and pressed the trigger again. The tool roared to life and spun against the surface of the tunnel. Kyle drilled for twenty seconds before he pulled the tool away to check his progress. He felt with his hand to see how deeply the diamond bit had penetrated the metal and couldn't find even a dent. He held up his silk blot to get more light and still couldn't see anything.

He picked the drill up again and put his body weight against it, holding down the trigger tightly. Kyle drilled again for over a minute. This time, though, he knew he wasn't making any progress because the bit kept slipping. He couldn't even get enough of a foothold with the diamond bit to keep the drill in one place. He pushed even harder, driving the drill against the metal, and tried for a few more seconds. Just as he was about to give up, the diamond drill bit snapped, falling with a *ping* to the floor of the tunnel near his knees.

"Dammit!" Kyle screamed. He wondered if Sillow had it completely wrong. *What if there's nothing out there? What if there's nothing I can do to stop this?* he wondered to himself.

He took the drill, and hurled it against the wall. He picked it up again and threw it in total frustration. This time, the drill broke into several pieces, one of them bouncing back and hitting Kyle in the face. He picked up one of the pieces of the drill's handle and threw it against the wall again. It felt good to destroy something.

"No!!!!" Kyle screamed again. "No!!" Screaming felt good too. "Dammit!" he yelled.

He turned around to head back toward 2017, dreading the fact that he had to tell Allaire what he'd found. He knew she'd be as devastated as he was. He wondered how he would tell her something he knew would destroy her . . .

"Shit," he screamed. He was still carrying the open backpack in his hand as he started moving in the tunnel. He grabbed for something to throw again, and found the wooden paddle with the ancient Serican writing on it. He turned toward the end of the tunnel again and flung the paddle as hard as he could. "Fuck you!" he screamed as he released the paddle, excited to see the wood shatter to pieces.

But, as the paddle flew through the air, it hit the top of the tunnel first, and then skidded through the air making a direct hit against the wall at the end. Instead of shattering, though, the paddle looked like it had done what the drill could not. Kyle moved closer to examine what he thought he was seeing, but was sure could not be possible. He saw that, indeed, the flimsy wooden paddle had torn a small, jagged line right through the top of the tunnel. What was even more amazing was that a small circle of daylight was creeping through. Kyle pressed his eye as close as he could to the hole in the tunnel's ceiling. He saw the sky, purplish, as if it was sunset, with gray clouds moving fast from left to right.

Then, he moved to the end of the tunnel again, toward a tiny pinhole in the wall, also caused by the paddle. Kyle pressed his eye against it but it was too small to see through.

He picked the paddle up from the floor of the tunnel and started chiseling against the pinhole. The metal of the tunnel responded like soft clay to Kyle's gentle hammering with the strange wooden paddle.

In less than a minute, Kyle opened up a hole in the tunnel the size of a fist. He couldn't explain how a small piece of wood could do what a drill with a diamond bit could not, but he smiled as he lowered his head to look through the hole.

He saw a long ditch up ahead of him, with mulberry bushes growing along the length of it. The sky was deep purple as if there were an extreme sunset, except the sun was high in the sky.

Kyle heard a rustling in the grass above the ditch and looked out the hole to his left where he saw a short man with a gray stubbly buzz cut. The man leaned against a rake he was holding and looked back at Kyle, wrinkling his brow, like he was trying to figure out whether what he was seeing was possible. The man started to walk away, then turned back to look again.

Kyle pulled away from the hole for a second.

"Hey!" the man screamed.

Kyle looked out again, but saw that the man wasn't calling for him, he was waving over someone else.

"Hey! Get over here! And get Simyon!" the man called out again.

In a matter of a few minutes, there were more than twenty people standing together looking at the hole. They each held a tool of some sort—a shovel, rake, wheelbarrow, or hedge clippers.

They were all dressed very simply, with both men and women in button-up shirts and baggy pants held up with suspenders. A man with a green silk handkerchief around his forehead walked up to the group and then stepped down into the ditch. He was now eye level with Kyle.

At first, the man had a slight smirk on his face. Then, as he walked toward Kyle, his smirk turned into more of a frown. He leaned closer to the hole, moving his face toward Kyle so quickly that it made Kyle jump backward.

Now, Kyle's heart was really racing. He leaned forward to the hole again and saw the man raise his arm into the air. He was holding a wooden paddle too—the same shape as Kyle's. Kyle flinched and moved backward when the man swung his paddle through the air and connected with the existing hole, chipping off another piece of the tunnel, enlarging the hole Kyle had started. The man swung again, and the hole got even bigger.

Kyle considered turning back and trying to get back to 2017 before the hole was big enough for him to get out—or them to get in. But, he needed the answers that could only be found beyond the tunnel. So, Kyle picked up his own paddle and started chipping away at the metal from his side as well.

The hole would be big enough to slip through in no time at all.

To be continued . . .